A Novel to Read on the Train

T0273027

Dumitru Tsepeneag

A NOVEL TO READ
ON THE TRAIN

Translated from the French by Alistair Ian Blyth

DALKEY ARCHIVE PRESS

Dallas / Dublin

Originally published in French by P.O.L as *Roman de gare* in 1985.

Copyright © by Dumitru Tsepeneag, 2021.
Translation copyright © by Alistair Ian Blyth, 2021.
First Dalkey Archive edition, 2021
All rights reserved.

CIP data

ROMANIAN
CULTURAL
INSTITUTE

Partially funded by the Translation Publication Support Program of
the Romanian Cultural Institute.

www.dalkeyarchive.com
Dallas / Dublin

Printed on permanent/durable acid-free paper.

Translator's Preface

A Novel to Read on the Train (*Roman de gare*, Éditions P.O.L., 1985) was the first novel that Dumitru Tsepeneag wrote in French, reluctantly recognizing that there was no prospect of him ever agaïn having a Romanian readership as long as his native country's communist régime endured. Having become a stateless exile in France after his citizenship was revoked by Nicolae Ceaușescu in 1975, previous to *A Novel to Read on the Train,* Tsepeneag had written three novels[1] for the sole reader that was his French translator, Alain Paruit, without any hope of the Romanian originals ever being published.

In French, a *roman de gare,* a "railway station novel," is a term for pulp fiction, the kind of schlock you buy on the station concourse to read on the train, the forerunner of the "airport novel," in other words. But Tsepeneag's novel is literally, ludically, a railway station novel, in that it is set in a railway station, where a hapless cast of actors

---

[1] *Arpièges* [Vain Art of the Fugue], trans. Alain Paruit, (Paris: Éditions Flammarion, 1973); *Les Noces nécessaires* [The Necessary Nuptials], trans. Alain Paruit, (Paris: Éditions Flammarion, 1977); *Le Mot sablier* [The Sandglass Hour], trans. Alain Paruit, (Paris: Éditions P.O.L., 1984).

and film crew are trying and failing to shoot an adapta-
tion of a novella set in a railway station. Although not
specifically stated in the novel, the novella in question is
Tsepeneag's "Waiting," an "oneirist" text that describes an
isolated and soon-to-be disused whistle-stop that serves
a *Zauberberg*-like sanatorium on the other side of a mys-
terious forest swarming with indeterminate creatures, a
place of now deep snow, now incessant drizzle that hovers
between dream and reality. In the novella, the stationmaster, finally abandoned by both pointsman and telegraph
operator, waits interminably, menaced by an escaped and
now preternaturally huge eagle, brought there in a cage as a
chick by a beautiful woman whose train had been delayed
at the whistle-stop by snowdrifts on the line and who spoke
no known language. These were the original oneiric matri-
ces that would structure *A Novel to Read on the Train*.

The novella "Waiting" was published in *România
Literară* magazine in October 1970 and was included in
Tsepeneag's third collection of short stories, published in
1971.[2] Which is to say, this was the year when the slim vol-
ume (111 pages), with a black-and-white reproduction of
René Magritte's *Le Mal du Pays* on the cover,[3] was printed.
But as Tsepeneag notes in a journal entry dated June 7,
1971, the book never left the printer's since the necessary
baksheesh had failed to be paid.[4] Not even by the beginning of the following year had the book become available:
on January 10, 1972, Tsepeneag attended the opening of

[2] *Așteptare* [Waiting], (Bucharest: Cartea Românească, 1971).

[3] The painting shows a winged man gazing over a parapet and a recumbent lion, a therio-
morphic dream image to be found in "Waiting" and other stories in the collection.

[4] Dumitru Tsepeneag, *Opere 3: Un român la Paris. Jurnal,* (Bucharest: Editura Tracus
Arte, 2016), 161.

the new Cartea Românească bookshop in Bucharest, where all the publisher's books were on sale, with the single, glaring exception of *Waiting*.[5] By March of the same year, it seems that copies were finally to be found at the Cartea Românească bookshop,[6] but they were quickly withdrawn from the shelves and the book effectively vanished, just as its author, by now a persona non grata for the communist authorities, was to vanish from Romanian literature until after the fall of the Ceaușescu régime.

"Waiting" may be said to be the masterpiece and culmination of the "structural oneirism" that Tsepeneag had been developing throughout the 1960s with poet Leonid Dimov (1926–1987), a theory and practice of writing that took the dream as its criterion (Tsepeneag) or legislation (Dimov), lucidly constructing not a text that describes a dream but one that is structurally analogous to it: "in oneiric literature, as I conceive it, the dream is not a source, nor is it an object of study; the dream is a *criterion*. The difference is fundamental: I do not narrate a dream (mine or anybody else's), but rather I attempt to construct a reality *analogous* to the dream."[7] "Waiting" not only represents oneiric images—the anima figure of the beautiful (Swedish?) woman on the stranded train, the inexorably growing eagle that threatens to blot out the sky, the primal, Piero di Cosimo–esque forest—but does so in a structurally oneiric way: with the (il)logic of a dream, events and situations constantly shift, double back on themselves,

[5] *Un român la Paris. Jurnal*, p. 280.

[6] Dumitru Țepeneag, *Prin gaura cheii. Proză scurtă*, ed. Nicolae Bârna (Bucharest: Editura Allfa, 2001), 509.

[7] Dumitru Tsepeneag, "În căutarea unei definiții," *Luceafărul*, no. 25 (June 22, 1968); *Opere 5. Texte teoretice, interviuri, note critice, "șotroane. 1966-1989* (Bucharest, Editura Tracus Arte, 2017), 46.

repeat themselves in a different, disorienting order. In *A Novel to Read on the Train*, "Waiting" becomes the oneiric urtext of the novel: fragments of Alain Paruit's translation[8] of the novella are interspersed throughout the novel, gradually increasing in length, pervading the text, as the fiction within the fiction of the dream text subsumes the "reality" of the framing fiction of the actors shooting a film based on an original text whose own reality, at the time when the novel was written, had been placed *sous rature*, being part of a book that had been disappeared and was therefore as insubstantial as a dream.

As *Roman de gare* progresses, the boundary between dream text and cinematic enactment thereof becomes blurred, and the director, who is also the author of the novella on which his film is based, increasingly loses control of his cast. Just as a dreamer has no control over the actions of the persons appearing in his dream, the director has increasingly little influence over his actors, who begin to act independently of him, in defiance of him, until finally he is reduced to a faint voice impotently crying "cut!" from the water closet, crucified by flatulence and diarrhea. In *Roman de gare*, the director—the author trapped within his own text like the director in the toilet cubicle—is analogous to a dreamer, who has no conscious control over his unfolding dream, while the real author, Dumitru Tsepeneag, stands outside the text, lucidly structuring it according to the principles of the dream.

In an important text of his 1960s oneirist period, "A Stage Production," published in the collection of short

---

[8] Dumitru Tsepeneag, *Exercices d'attente*, trans. Alain Paruit (Paris: Flammarion, 1972).

stories *Cold* (1967),[9] Tsepeneag had already explored the actor's defiance of his director, the fictional character's independence from his narrator. In the novella, the author/director enlists the habitués of a disreputable tavern, the bohemian occupants of his tenement house, and a girl inveigled to abscond from boarding school in a reenactment of the Nativity and Crucifixion, in which a bicycle pump will stand in for the Holy Ghost. The three-part novella was published in *Gazeta Literară*, no. 40 (779), October 5, 1967, but only the first part was subsequently included in *Cold*, the second and third parts having been censored in the meantime. (In the second part, "The Passion of a Playwright," the author, who has been appealing for the institution of a "new theater"—a new fictional dispensation, an oneiric ontology of fiction—is literally crucified by his characters during the performance of his text, egged on by the audience, and in the third part, "Epilogue," the subsequent Ascension consists of the author escaping the country by helicopter. Neither of which themes was congenial to an atheist, closed-border, totalitarian society.) The two Marias of "A Stage Production," representing the Virgin Mary and Mary Magdalene, were to recur in *Vain Art of the Fugue* (1973), in the form of the oneirically interchangeable Maria and Magda, and later in a screenplay entitled *The Two Marias*, which Tsepeneag wrote before *Roman de gare*, but which was never produced or published. Fragments of the screenplay are interspersed throughout *A Novel to Read on the Train,* adding yet another intratextual oneiric layer—a text that exists only as a dream of itself within another text.

---

[9] *Frig* (Bucharest: Editura..., 1967).

At the end of *Roman de gare*, a first-person narrator recounts watching the very film whose failed production the novel has hitherto been representing as it is subsumed by the oneiric urtext of "Waiting." The film will recur in Tsepeneag's later novels *Hotel Europa* (1996), *Pont des Arts* (1998), and *La Belle Roumaine* (2004), where it will be watched by yet other characters who have escaped the control of their narrator and exerted their own separate metaphysical reality, like persons occurring in a dream.[10] Through *A Novel to Read on the Train*, "Waiting" becomes an endlessly self-replicating text, linking together the whole of Tsepeneag's work, which may thus be read as an unfolding dream of textual dreams within dreams. And ultimately, this is the achievement of Tsepeneag's practice as a writer and as a theorist of writing: the lucid recognition that dreams and texts are different but structurally analogous aspects of a single reality—that the two have more in common with each other than they do with the "real world."

---

[10] "La vue en rêve d'une personne est, à certains points de vue, une preuve de sa réalité métaphysique," Giorgio de Chirico, *L'Art métaphysique*, ed. Giovanni Lista (Paris: l'Échoppe, 1994), 60.

A Novel to Read on the Train

A MAN IS ASLEEP.

His eyes are closed, but his face, in close-up, is more like that of somebody waiting, somebody lying in wait. Maybe he isn't asleep. Maybe he's pretending.

Pan back to reveal the bed, the body lying as if on a stretcher. Or better said, as if in a coffin. His hands are folded crosswise over his chest, on top of the rose-madder coverlet. Alongside the bed is a bare wall.

Now the man's eyes are open, and the impression that he is waiting becomes even stronger. We follow his eyes as they travel from right to left.

On the bedside table are sundry items: a button, a fountain pen, a whistle, an alarm clock, an eraser, a wrist-watch, a photograph in which we can make out a youngish woman. Later, we shall see her in the flesh.

Pan to the window. The ticking of the clock is the only sound.

Through the window we can see a small village square, in the middle of which there is a monument portraying victorious soldiers bearing aloft an eagle with outspread wings.

Jean C. lights a cigarette. He takes a drag. The taste is bitter. He doesn't like smoking on an empty stomach. He could do with a cup of coffee, perhaps also a croissant. But for that he will have to go downstairs.

The small square in the sunlight.

The character now stands before the mirror set above the washbasin. He looks as fresh as a daisy. He brushes his teeth, gargles. He opens the wardrobe to take out his uniform. He gets dressed.

He puts on a necktie.

He goes out.

Jean C. wouldn't mind going out either.

He walks along the hotel corridor. He comes to a stop in front of a door and knocks a couple of times. No answer from within. He opens the door a crack. In the semidarkness can be descried the outline of a woman lying on a bed. Her lower half, to be precise.

Jean C. stands motionless for a few seconds. The rustle of leaves. As if people were walking through a forest. He doesn't get it right away. Now he does. He softly closes the screenplay folder. He puts the fountain pen and the eraser in his pocket, fastens the watch around his wrist. The strap is tight. Like a garrote, he thinks.

He goes out, head bowed.

The hotel corridor is dimly lit. He looks at his feet, the toes of his shoes, the red, threadbare carpet. His gait is hesitant. He comes to a stop in front of a door, runs his hand over his brow, takes a deep breath, puffing out his chest, continues on his way. He descends the flight of stairs to the bistro. Mind the narrow, slippery steps. Downstairs, somebody is busy behind the bar.

He orders a coffee. Strong. With a dash of milk? He doesn't answer right away. He walks across the room to the entrance and looks at his watch. No milk. Thanks. He goes up to the bar. The zinc countertop is too high for him to lean his elbows on it. He asks for a croissant, no, better a brioche. The others are fast asleep. He takes another look at his watch: true, it's a little early. His coffee is served. He sips it. He smacks his lips in satisfaction, clicks his tongue. But then, all of a sudden, he appears to be in a rush: he takes a bite of the brioche, hurriedly chomps it, drains the cup of coffee in one gulp, and, pocketing the rest of the roll, climbs the stairs.

Back in his room, he sets about reading once more. What a drag!

If you were to ask him why he agreed to play the part, what could he say? That he found the director an agreeable sort of guy . . . Despite his patronising tone and foreign accent, which he endeavored to smother in booze, to disguise, amid the belches, grunts, and belly gurgles which, that evening, provided an accompaniment to the ingurgitation of gallons of red: white wine is for matutinal tipplers, for gurning gatekeepers, for girls on the game, for café garçons getting on in years. Look at how lovely the colour is! Like the gore of a Bulgarian lying with his gullet gashed in a station waiting room . . . None too glib, are you? Nothing to say, eh? I love your dogged silence, your guileless poise, your fishlike eyes . . . You piss your pants and sit there calmly as the puddle spreads. You're not given to fidgeting, unlike some!

Having given the foregoing rant, he inserted the thumb of his left hand in his mouth and with it rubbed his teeth. His other hand grasped his glass. There was no gainsaying his elated garrulousness . . . He continued: Go on, drink, guzzle the precious liquid, stationmaster, gargle it, *chef de gare*, and grin forlornly the way only you know how . . .

His gob was in full spate, the bugger! But he was good at it, he knew how to flatter without making it obvious and always at the right moment, just when you were most susceptible. A real brownnoser!

Except that now, with the script in front of him, it's no longer going to wash. Try to get into it, make an effort, come on!

The stationmaster limbers up with a few morning exercises. He goes to the washbasin, looks in the mirror, gives himself a wink of merry complicity. He brushes his teeth, gargles, spits noisily. He grimaces: a tooth gives a twinge, a molar. He takes off his pajamas. He is now in just his undervest. He brushes his teeth.

Jean takes a bite of his brioche.

He looks out of the window again: it's raining.

He gets dressed. He puts on a carefully ironed white shirt, a brand-new uniform, a well-brushed cap. He knots his necktie. The necktie is red, the same as the cap. He smiles.

The stationmaster sits down in an armchair. He sits there without budging for quite a few minutes in a row. He looks at the photograph, which is still on the bedside table.

He goes to the window: it is no longer raining. He sits back down in the armchair. He stares into space.

The stationmaster, now in bed, pretends to sleep. A blank wall.

He gets out of bed, goes to the window: it's raining. He is wearing long johns and an undervest.

Looking into the mirror above the washbasin. He smiles.

Jean finishes his brioche, munching briskly.

The stationmaster shaves. Lathers his face thickly. He is having fun.

No, start all over again, take it from the top. Jean C. sits down on the bed, holding the burgundy folder. He crosses his legs: I need to read it patiently. Professionally.

I fall asleep.

In close-up, my face is sooner that of somebody waiting, somebody lying in wait. Settled. Maybe I'm not asleep. Maybe I'm pretending. Should I then open my eyes or just bat my eyelashes? I make my eyelashes flutter. Imperceptibly. The camera is focused on my face. Only then do you see the bed and, naturally, the rest of my body, lying as if on a stretcher. He's reluctant to say coffin. That's up to him! Moving on: the hands folded over the chest, the red coverlet, etcetera.

My eyes are open. The impression that I'm waiting is now even stronger. My eyes travel from right to left. The reader's from left to right!

I look at the sundry items to be found on the bedside table: a button, a whistle, an alarm clock, a photograph. It's of Marie-Christine, naturally.

By rights, this bit is the cameraman's job, likewise all the stuff that comes next: the small village square, the monument that doesn't yet exist, the hills. The sun.

Back in the bedroom. In front of the mirror above the sink, I attempt to knot my necktie, without success. And I give up. I shrug. I step over to the cupboard, open it, look for something inside. I don't find what I'm looking for. I take the signalman's flag that pokes from the neck of an empty calvados bottle. And here, with that accent of his, or rather without any accent, since he only has a single word, he will shout: "Cut!"

I then walk down the corridor, holding the flag. I stop before a door and knock two or three times. No answer.

I open the door a crack. I don't like peering through key-holes. But even so, I drop to a crouch. I bend my knees. I glimpse the body of a woman stretched out on the bed. Is she wearing a nightdress? Is she stark naked? This needs to be specified. You can barely see her and it's hard to make out the details. Her head isn't visible. I remain motionless for a few seconds. I hear a rustle of leaves. It's not me who hears it, obviously. It can be heard . . . As if some people were walking through a forest. All well and good. Perfect up to this point. I softly close the door. I walk away, head bowed.

In the next shot, I'm coming down the stairs. A charac-ter named Jean asks the highly important question: "How's it going?" I beg your pardon: it's me who asks the question, after bidding him a good morning, and he replies that it's going all right, and then asks me how it's going, and, looking rather preoccupied, I say that, yes, it's going all right. I'm so preoccupied that I fail to answer straightaway when he asks whether I would like coffee or tea. In fact, no, before that I walk across the bistro to the front door and look up at the sky. I say: "You know, it's not all that early . . ." And I go outside.

"Meh!" exclaims the barkeeper, gesticulating and gri-macing for emphasis, and then opens the front door of the bistro to watch as the stationmaster walks into the distance. We view him from behind. His gait is leisurely. He meets two peasants coming the other way. One of them has a lamb cradled in his arms. The peasants greet the stationmaster, and he returns their greeting.

It is spring. Fine weather.

A goods train passes through the station. The station-master—me, in other words—stands on the platform: I lower the flag and look to my left. My arm aches slightly. The switchman, who also acts as the small station's storeman, idly trails a broom over the platform. He is quite short, shorter even than I am. His bearded face is comical and wild at the same time. He looks like a Japanese actor whose name I forget. He casts me a furtive glance and picks up his pace. He is now making jerky, Chaplinesque movements. I walk over to him with seemingly menacing tread. Still avoiding my eyes, he moves away. The scene needs to be comical. I bet it will require multiple takes . . .

The telegraphist appears in the doorway of the telegraph office. He has long blond hair. He watches the scene with obvious amusement. You get the distinct feeling that the same scene is repeated every morning.

The stationmaster turns to the telegraphist.

STATIONMASTER
How's it going, Thomas?

THOMAS
All right, boss. The slow train's going to be late. They just announced it.

STATIONMASTER
(*muttering to himself*)
That's too bad . . .

The switchman seizes the opportunity to vanish behind the clump of peonies and rosebushes planted in front of the storeroom. The stationmaster looks around after him. But he isn't genuinely annoyed.

STATIONMASTER
Where in God's name has he got to?

Thomas looks right and left. There is nobody to be seen.
The stationmaster smiles, satisfied, so it would seem, at
how things have turned out. Got it! I need to come across
like a father amused at the antics of his young son. All
right then. Why not?

THOMAS
He's scarpered.

STATIONMASTER
Yeah, right . . .
(*pause*)
Oh well.

He makes a meaningful gesture. But what kind of
gesture?
I shake my head, give a chuckle. Thomas does likewise;
his chuckle is rather forced. I take two steps toward the
railway line. Thomas continues to laugh inanely. Gradually,
his laughter becomes less and less forced. I come to a stop.
I prick up my ears. The wind. Forest noises (this will be a
constant part of the soundtrack). After a few seconds, off
camera, the sound of a tap running and glasses tinkling.
The intent expression on the stationmaster's face.
I have my own little device for this bit: with the tip of
my tongue I stroke the remains of a molar that cracked
long ago and which I am reluctant to entrust to the den-
tist's pliers. I brush it regularly, three times a day. I carefully
tend it. That molar is my special tool.

SHE'S JUST WOKEN up. She stretches, yawns. Tenses her arms, her legs. Then spreads them. She sprawls with visible pleasure. Turns on her side. For a moment she thinks about going back to sleep. Closes her eyes. Moves her lips. Moistens them with her tongue. A taste rather like sperm. The way some men's sperm tastes, that is. A minute's reflection on this subject, although there's not all that much that can be drawn from it; basically, the truth of the matter must have to do with chemistry.

Marie-Christine B. opens one eye and pricks up her ears. Somebody is knocking on the door. That somebody then presses the door handle. The door softly opens a crack. The woman does not ask who is there, nor can she see who it is, because her bed is in the corner that the opening door occludes. The inquisitive somebody closes the door and goes away. His footsteps sound hesitant.

She sits up in bed. The coverlet slides down, revealing her naked chest. She yawns. She feels her breasts. To be more exact, she hoists them, weighs them, like a breastfeeding mother checking her milk reserves.

She gets out of bed. She has a large bottom. Powerful buttocks. She swings her arms. Her boobs jiggle.

She goes over to the sink, looks at herself in the mirror attentively: she is rather satisfied with what she sees. She brushes her teeth. She combs her blond hair, tying it into a

bun at the back of her neck. She goes to the window, opens
the shutters: the small village square in the rain.

She gets dressed. Opens the door of the cupboard to
look for something. She doesn't find it. She bends down
to look under the bed. There it is, the blessed burgundy
folder . . . And now, to work!

Last night, she was unable to do any reading at all.
Because of him. That director can be a pain in the arse
sometimes! Just like all beginners. Pushy, garrulous, nit-
picking, and to top it all, he even tried to come on to
her. Bashfully, awkwardly. Or else he thought it somehow
refined. "You do realize," said he, straining to conceal his
accent, "you are a strong woman, a beautiful woman, a
woman with a capital W . . . It's thanks to you that the
village lives in peace, that harmony reigns . . . Marie means
'to love,' it's an anagram of *aimer*!"

"Don't bust a blood vessel, I've read it all in the synopsis
already," said she. He looked at her as if she had just said
something vulgar. She felt obliged to give him a friendly
pat on the arm. "Don't take it so hard, old man, carry
on." Meanwhile, Jean C. was staring at a fixed point on
the wall, his mouth clenched solemnly. He is going to be
perfect for the rôle, which fits him like a glove.

"A tin glove," he quipped.

And what about her rôle? What does she think of it?

You should always look the director straight in the eye,
especially when he asks you a superfluous question like
that.

Was he trying to hoodwink her already?

"I'm not asking you whether you like the part. I assume
you do, since you accepted it . . . I simply want to know

what you think of it." And again that naïve look of his. False or genuine, there was no way of knowing, because at times there was a fleeting, malicious gleam in his eye. There was no way of knowing how far he was prepared to go with the disdain for his actors that every self-respecting director has to cultivate on set. You look him straight in the eyes, but see nothing there . . . His power resides precisely in the uncertainty in which he is able to envelop himself, in the curiosity that is aroused all by itself, the curiosity to which only someone like Jean C. is immune. It resides in his power of seduction.

This having been said, she likes her rôle, her double rôle. She tucks the script under her arm and decides to go downstairs for a coffee: a double espresso.

She sits down at a table with a large cup in front of her and starts to read.

The face of the stationmaster, while eating. The sound of running water and tinkling glasses.

Two peasants are talking at another table. The muzzle of a lamb peeps out from underneath the table. The viewpoint is from behind the bar, where a woman still young is doing the dishes. She is in very good spirits.

MARIE
Like it?

STATIONMASTER
(*with his mouth full*)
Fabulous!

The woman addresses somebody coming down the stairs.

MARIE
What about you? Aren't you hungry? Get yourself down
here already. Hup!

She banters, washing the dishes all the while. A small
bearded man has come to a stop halfway down the stairs.
He looks at her. He stretches, gives a lascivious yawn. No,
that doesn't work. It's a little bit silly.

MARIE
Are you coming downstairs or not? Come on . . .

I feel like reading that line out loud: "Are you coming
downstairs or not? Come on . . ." One of the peasants calls
out: "Say it louder!" The other one bursts out laughing.
They're making fun of me. But it doesn't matter. Back to
work. I have to come across as carefree.
One of the peasants calls out.

PEASANT
Say it louder!

SECOND PEASANT
Gosh!

The stationmaster eats quickly, his mind elsewhere.
Marc, the switchman, comes up to the bar and orders a
drink.

MARC
A large glass.

MARIE
Aren't you eating first?

MARC
Hurry up with that red!

MARIE
Aren't you going to have a bite?

But I serve him the drink anyway. He knocks the wine back, wipes his mouth with the back of his hand and, without the slightest hesitation, heads for the door at the back of the bistro. Meanwhile, the peasants continue to banter. They gesticulate copiously. At intervals, the lamb attempts to get out from underneath the table, but every time the two peasants push it back under quite violently.

"It's been a long time . . ." says one of them, loudly enough for everybody else to hear.

"You mean . . ."

Later, in Thomas's room. I go to the window. In bed, the blond telegraph operator shows signs of impatience.

THOMAS
Are you coming to bed?

I look out of the window at the small square with its monument. Its invisible monument!

It's raining. A summer rain. A shower. It will soon stop. The stationmaster walks through the rain. He heads toward the bistro. I look at the bed, where Thomas, beneath the cover, is fiddling with himself. He's sick of waiting for me. I smile. I have to be smilingly serene all the time.

Another coffee?

I've had enough of this; the dialogue is utterly stupid. Out of the question! But it's like that deliberately, he will say. Then what? Deliberate stupidity . . .

I drink a second cup of coffee and head toward the door at the back. The garden side. Behind the honeysuckle bushes, a plain stretches as far as the eye can see. The sun is shining. The birds are twittering. The cows are grazing. The director is lying on the grass, his belly turned skyward. He stretches, yawns.

I raise one arm to shield my eyes from the sun. I pretend not to have seen him. Perhaps he hasn't seen me either.

Peace and harmony. The honeysuckle smells good. Quite some distance away, the director of photography and the cameraman are setting up the camera. There are also a few sheep.

HE HAS CALLED them all together in the dining room of the bistro.

They need to discuss the script some more, the better to understand, not the meaning, the direction—what direction? It's got nothing to do with any direction, they're not rolling down a highway . . .

"The direction of the hands going round a clock," somebody suggests, and the director gives him an outraged, offended look, unless he is just pretending, and says:

"Never mind the direction! It's all to do with the ambiance, the overall atmosphere, which isn't always the same. At the beginning, or in the first part of the film anyway, you see that a kind of harmony reigns in the village, in the café on the square, or the bistro, if you prefer. And all thanks to Marie. It's thanks to her that the village dwells in tranquility. The men drink, play dice, chat peacefully, and then make love to Marie or mostly just fondle her . . ."

"We get all that!"

"Even the switchman, the most restless of the characters, finds soothing moments in her company. For example, they occasionally watch TV . . . The two of them . . ."

"We know!"

"Let him speak, for God's sake!"

"This carefree life is one evening turned upside down

by the arrival of another woman, who takes a room for the night. She says she will only be staying the one night, before travelling on to the sanatorium on the other side of the hill, in the middle of the forest."

The director points his arm in the direction of the open door. It's hot. The sound engineer comes in by the back door, causing the company's eyes to move from one door to the other. Marie-Christine takes advantage of this brief moment of confusion to order a cup of coffee.

The director falls silent. In front of him he has a number of typewritten pages, probably the synopsis, as well as some handwritten notes. He looks through them, not seeming to find what he is looking for, and ends up reading a different paragraph from the synopsis.

"Marie feels more and more attracted to the newcomer, whose first name is also Marie and who looks very much like her."

"Six and two threes!"

"Are the two Maries married?" asks a wise guy.

"Let him speak!"

The director asks a question.

"Have you all read the script?"

The chorus of voices can hardly say otherwise than that yes, they have. But the director has his doubts as to this answer, which sounds too categorical to be true. In a sulky voice he starts to say something like this: "The relationship between the two women is obviously . . ." But he leaves it hanging mid-sentence, no doubt conscious that the tautology is ultimately too much to take, even if it does form the basis of the logic.

"We've read the script, says Marie-Christine B.," in a voice of perfect calmness. And assurance.

"So, I wanted to talk to you about the atmosphere . . . Or rather the change in the atmosphere after a certain point in the film . . . after the arrival of the second Marie. But I see that it's perfectly clear to you all."

"Yes!" exclaims the chorus.

"You've read the synopsis, you've read the script . . ."

He pauses. Yes, it would seem that everybody has read the synopsis, everybody has read the script. So much the better!

"In any event, the action is simple, it doesn't pose any difficulty. It needs to be kept simple in order to be effective . . ."

Having got that out of the way, from his pocket he takes a book, which he shows them with an air of slight embarrassment.

"This book contains a novella I published a long time ago."

He has begun to speak more loudly. In his raised hand they can see a grubby, well-thumbed book with a blue and white cover. He continues:

"It's the starting point for our film. Or at least . . . to tell the truth, the starting point is even farther back . . ."

"At birth," whispers Marie-Christine in a mellow voice, apparently without any trace of irony.

So why do they all turn their heads to look at her?

A rather heavy silence ensues. Fortunately, the director finds a comeback to her remark, saying:

"Don't joke about it, because it's true. It's almost true . . ."

The tension dissolves, they find their tongues, even start making wisecracks. It's better this way, think Jean C. and Marie-Christine B. almost in the same instant.

"An unhappy childhood!"

"A smacked botty!"

"Not at all. Just the opposite."

"A happy one, then!"

"Yes, ladies and gentlemen, a happy one. As far as I can recall!"

"Memories alter over time."

The director is determined to stand up to them:

"That's why we make films . . ."

"Waiter, another glass!"

"A glass of white for me!"

He stands up, rather pale-faced, but his hand doesn't shake when he gestures for silence, and they comply, lowering their voices, eventually falling silent.

"I can see that you're almost there in your understanding of it. And so tomorrow we shall begin."

"Filming? Already?"

"Not exactly . . . First of all rehearsals, tests. Let's get to work!"

He puts the book back in his pocket, shuffles together his pages, but does not make his exit. It's his duty always to be present. Omnipresent, even. He almost smiles when he sits down at Jean C. and Marie-Christine B.'s table. He orders himself a drink.

"Don't take it to heart," says Jean C., although it is unclear to whom, because he has his nose in his glass, and with the nail of his left index finger he is scraping a wine stain on the tablecloth.

"The essential thing is to make the film," observes Marie-Christine B. philosophically.

"It's what we're here for," mutters the director.

"What I mean is that you've managed the hardest part," adds the actress.

"The money?"

"Too right. That's no mean feat . . ."

"It's amazing, you mean?"

"Why amazing?"

Their tone of voice has grown friendlier. The director offers to buy another round.

"This one's on the boss."

He is now completely relaxed. If they want to talk about the budget, that's just fine. But nevertheless, there's one thing that needs to be clarified in advance.

"Let's not get carried away: the budget is quite modest."

"Not all that modest."

"Right. But even so . . ."

"The film board was quite generous."

"Yes, it was."

"You can't complain."

"I'm not complaining."

Just to keep the conversation going, the actress asks to see the dog-eared book the director showed them a little earlier.

"Let's have a look at your booklet," says she.

She takes no notice of the author's embarrassment as he displays his opus. "You're either an exhibitionist or you aren't," she thinks to herself, by way of justification. But now that she has got her hands on the book, she too is gripped by a certain embarrassment. She handles it coyly, awkwardly. She weighs it in her hand.

"It's not weighty."

She flicks through it, comes to a stop at a page describing

an eagle which, having been freed from its cage, has started growing uncontrollably. She lowers her head and reads:

Above the forest, the sky turned crimson and, after a while, the eagle burst forth, as big as an airplane, and began to fly above the station in broad circles, broader and broader.

"They're my old short stories," says the man whose name is inscribed on the front cover.

"Will we have to read them?" asks Jean C. in an anxious voice, and all three burst into laughter.

"Waiter, another round."

The book vanishes back inside the director's deep pocket.

Ultimately, it's not the budget that Marie-Christine is interested in. She feels hot. She unbuttons her blouse a little lower. She drains her glass and then asks a subtle, even a delicate question:

"Tell me: what would you have done if you hadn't got the advance?"

"The advance on box office takings?"

"Yes."

The director hesitates for a moment. Jean C. is looking at him, too. With his round, moist eyes.

"I don't really understand your question . . ."

Obviously, he's trying to buy time. He is afraid of giving an honest answer. He sips his wine. He takes out a handkerchief to wipe his mouth. He sees very well that their curiosity is only growing the keener. Now he is cornered. Nothing for it!

"I would have written a novel. Quite simply . . ."

The actress seems satisfied with what she takes to be the frankness of this answer. She stares at the director, at this man whom she doesn't really know: up until two months ago, she had never met him, never even heard of him. She gives his arm a friendly pat, as if to encourage him to carry on being frank.

"Not a bad idea. Not bad at all. You can still do it," she says, with a look half-lascivious, half-tender.

THE WINDOW. IT's stopped raining. I look out of the window. A peasant with a flock of sheep crosses the village square. Leaving the bistro, Marc bumps into the peasant, who is very tall. Very tall and thin. They shake hands, gesticulate. The switchman extends his arm in the direction of the station. They are standing next to the monument (which, for the time being, does not exist). It's something to do with the station. To avoid any misunderstanding, Marc imitates a locomotive: he jerks his arms like pistons, he whistles. He does so quite a few times. That's enough! The other man understands perfectly. The train enters the station. Obviously! They both laugh, splitting their sides. It even makes me feel like laughing.

In front of the mirror, I'm still smiling. I ought to shave. I shrug my shoulders. I try to knot my necktie, don't manage it, toss the necktie on the bed.

The door opens.

MARIE
You're going to be late.

She goes straight back out again.
I need to hurry. To take long strides down the hallway.
"Action!"

I take long strides down the hallway. Drat! I stumble, totter, almost lose my balance.

"Cut!"

The director seems happy with it. He says it will do, no reason why not, but then, at the insistence of the camera-man, we do another take. Two takes, even. A completely insignificant scene. More a camera test than a real scene.

"All right, now get out of here!" says the cameraman. He wants to film the empty corridor. Since we're here anyway.

"You get on my nerves," says the director.

Marie-Christine gives a gurgling chuckle. She has to keep up the cheeriness constantly, poor woman.

She claps me on both shoulders.

"Get out of the shot," yells the cameraman.

We all go downstairs. It's quite busy in the bistro. I've brought the script with me and, tucked between the pages, the signals flag.

"He's never parted with it," somebody quips.

"It's his job, after all," says another.

They're in the mood for some comedy, and I'm the straight man.

I arrive on the platform all out of breath: with my boot-laces still untied, carelessly dressed, not wearing a necktie, my cap askew.

I wave my flag. The local train pulls into the station. It has only three carriages, of the old-fashioned sort.

Two people get off the train. One is cradling a lamb. Marc greets them warmly. They shake hands. The switch-man teases the lamb, which bleats.

Meanwhile, another passenger alights. It's Mathieu, the singer. The train pulls out of the station. I give a respectful salute, even slightly overdoing it. Flag raised.

Only now do I notice Mathieu and I go up to him.

STATIONMASTER
Had a good journey?

MATHIEU
Yes, very good. Even managed to have a nap . . . Almost
missed my stop.

He has a shrill voice. Gesticulates a lot. The same as
Marc, who now comes up to us, with the two peasants.
The lamb bleats. Thomas also comes over. Mathieu lights
a cigarette, which he grips between his thumb and index
finger.
The camera pans back. We can no longer hear what
they are saying, but merely see them from afar, as part of
the landscape.
Then we see them from the other side of the tracks,
with the station behind them, etcetera.
They leave the platform and head for the bistro.
I remain on the platform. Mathieu turns his head to
look at me.

MATHIEU
Aren't you coming?

STATIONMASTER
I'll be there a little later . . .

MATHIEU
See you!

STATIONMASTER
See you!

Mathieu lengthens his stride to catch up with the small group of people crossing the square. They pass close by the monument. Close by the spot where it is supposed to be. They stop for a moment, talking loudly. Mathieu stubs out the rest of his cigarette. He grinds it with his heel. The director raises his arms.

"Let's not go over the top, there's only so much we can film . . . And that's that."

"We're not filming, we're going round in circles."

"That's none of your business!"

"No, it isn't, but why are we rehearsing scenes that we can't film?"

"That's right! What's the point rehearsing?"

"We're rehearsing because you need to rehearse. That's why!"

Another two people come up and join the group. They all slowly move off in the direction of the bistro, which also serves as a hotel. The sign is plain to see:

THE IMPERIAL EAGLE

As for me, of course, I merely watch as they walk away. I remain on the platform, head bowed, absorbed in my own thoughts. It's true: the whole business about the monument has been irritating everybody. Yesterday evening, to get out of the situation, the director (but is he the one to blame?) said, "Who gives a damn about the monument? We can live very well without the monument." We can die very well without it, he meant . . .

But in the end, why not? In which case, we also ought to dispense with the hotel sign.

"That's not the same thing at all."

"True, all too true . . ."

So, I've been left all alone on the platform. Holding the flag, as ever. I start walking, come to a stop, look in the direction of the forest, listen. The wind. The noise of the forest, growing louder. I stubbornly look straight ahead. I reach a decision: I cross the tracks. The edge of the forest is very close to the railroad line. But I come to a stop once more. As if not daring to go farther.

The camera alone keeps going. . .

"Wait a moment, I don't really understand this bit."

"The camera alone keeps going, that is, it moves past the stationmaster and goes searching among the trees. It's very clear! It's not your viewpoint this time."

"Then whose viewpoint is it?"

"It's an objective viewpoint . . ."

Birdsong. Rustling leaves. Through the trees we see four men carrying a stretcher.

"Carrying a what?"

"A very brief shot. After the men leave the frame, we see nothing but the trees, and on the soundtrack, the noise of the forest is louder than before. But that doesn't really concern you. Next!"

"All right, agreed, but look here."

"Where?"

"Here. Hey, waiter, another glass! Here! For a few seconds, we see a man walking on his own along a path in the forest. He looks carefree. At first sight, you might think he is the stationmaster, on his way back to the station. Can you see where?"

"Yes, but read the next bit. In reality . . ."

"What reality?"

"In reality, the stationmaster is still there, not far from the tracks, motionless, looking."

"I don't get it. Waiter! Where's that glass of mine!"

"There's nothing to get . . . For God's sake! As Godard would say."

"Godard?"

"Yes, Godard. Jean-Luc."

"I'm thirsty."

"Listen, Jean. Make an effort to understand that there's nothing to understand."

"Nothing?"

"Yes, nothing . . ."

"Waiter!"

"Waiter!!"

The director bangs his fist on top of the script. He then reads aloud from it. Because of his accent, some of the words are hard to make out . . .

From time to time the lamb tries to get out from under the table . . . No, further on! The men enter the bistro. They're all talking at once. Jean's good cheer adds to the general din. No, that's not it, he flicks to a few pages further on. They're laughing. All these snatches of conversation are more or less drowned out by the voices of the others, who are saying more or less the same thing. It's obvious that the words themselves are of no importance.

JEAN
Where has the stationmaster got to?

MATHIEU
He'll be along in a minute.

He pauses to drink, but his glass is empty.

"Listen to this bit:

"The stationmaster is all alone on the platform. Holding the flag. He walks a few steps, head bowed, stops, looks in the direction of the forest, strains to hear. The wind. The noise of the forest, growing louder.

"The stationmaster reaches a decision: he crosses the tracks. He stops. He looks in the direction of the forest. He takes another few steps. The edge of the forest is very close to the railroad line. But he comes to a stop once more. As if not daring to go farther."

"Waiter!"

The director is now standing up, holding the burgundy folder. He recites:

"Only the camera keeps going, it moves past the stationmaster and goes searching among the trees. Birdsong. Rustling leaves. Through the trees we see four men carrying a stretcher. A very brief shot. So brief the audience might even miss it."

He pauses. He looks at me, a strange light glimmering in his eyes. I turn my head and call for the waiter yet again, who seems overwhelmed. He's probably right, there's nothing here to understand . . . And anyway, why should I care! He's the director; he's the boss.

He continues reading.

"Toward the end of the scene, the noise of the forest blends into a hum of voices: the voices in the bistro, growing louder and louder. Everybody is talking at the same time. A real uproar. Somebody gets up and puts a coin in the jukebox."

The waiter finally arrives with another glass. I drain it in one gulp. When all is said and done, he's right. And besides, he can do whatever he likes in the cutting room. In there, he's completely in charge. But right now, it's difficult for him to carry on reading. He breaks off reading altogether. He sits down and looks around for his glass. He's thirsty. I say the words "cutting room" and he nods his head. He then grips his left earlobe, rubs it, tugs it, until it turns red. In a more relaxed voice he asks me whether I would like another glass, and I can't say no. I call the waiter.

Mathieu, Marc, and Thomas come over to our table, each holding a glass. They are in high spirits. The only thing bothering them is the monument, and to prove it, they bring it up again.

"It ought to be in place already," says Mathieu.

"Stop thinking about it," replies the director, rather curtly.

"And what about the eagle's cage?" asks Marc.

The director continues to twiddle his ear. He makes no reply.

"Let's drink," I say, aware that the conversation is about to take an unpleasant turn. But I can't help adding: "This curiosity of yours is quite unhealthy, sonny."

Marc looks at me in surprise. No doubt he's forgotten he's supposed to be my son. In which case, let him take it as just familiar talk over a glass of wine. But even so, he plays along.

"You're talking rubbish, Dad. Isn't he, boss? You can't claim that the cage isn't indispensable. Can he, boss?"

But the director says nothing. With his right thumb he rubs his teeth. With his other hand he twiddles his earlobe. Obviously, with him doing that, it's hard for him to answer.

Marie has just joined us. She is wearing a flowery skirt and a baggy shirt, half-unbuttoned. She smiles. She turns a chair around and straddles it, resting her hands and chin on the backrest.

"Better order a whole bottle," she suggests, looking at our empty glasses. "And an extra glass for me!"

When she raises her voice, her tone becomes a little unpleasant. It's as if her voice becomes strangulated, making it difficult for her to get the words out. This is why she is on the verge of giving up theatre. She's been doing theatre more and more seldom.

The bottle arrives. We fill our glasses, drink. Mathieu smokes. The director gazes at Marie-Christine as if with renewed interest. His gaze is almost naïve. After a few moments of this, Marie-Christine turns slightly to one side. But on the other side, she falls under the gaze of Marc, who stares at her breasts. She obviously feels ill at ease. To disguise her embarrassment, she turns her chair the right way around and says she feels hungry.

And it's true, we're all feeling hungry. The director is hungry too. He is looking at us more benignly than before.

"We'll have lunch We need to keep our strength up. It's going to be hard work this afternoon," he adds, in a paternal voice.

We don't need to pay attention. I look him straight in the eye and, keeping my own face perfectly blank, I say to myself: We don't need to pay attention to his antics, he's acting out a comic rôle of his own, albeit off-screen.

I GET DRESSED: a flowery skirt, quite loud, and a man's shirt, very large. No bra.

I open the cupboard, don't find what I'm looking for, look under the bed. There it is . . . Blasted script! I pick it up: it's falling apart, some of the pages are crumpled, others are probably missing . . . I couldn't care less. In any event, I can't be bothered to read the whole thing all in one go. I'll read it as we go along, during filming. And since there's nothing much to learn by heart . . . At least that's one advantage of cinema!

I tuck the script under my arm and go downstairs. I'm a little late. Everybody is in the bistro already. They're all talking at the same time. A terrible din. Music: some kind of foxtrot that was probably last fashionable just after the war. The stationmaster is sitting at a table with two peasants, playing dice. One of the peasants has a lamb under his arm.

STATIONMASTER
Put that lamb under the table. It's getting on my nerves.

He speaks in a calm but commanding voice. The peasant obeys. He puts the lamb under the table. The lamb bleats in protest.

PEASANT
Your turn. Throw!

STATIONMASTER
No, it's your turn . . .

The peasant casts the dice onto the baize.
At the bar, Mathieu is talking to Jean. They whisper and keep looking in the direction of the stationmaster, who casts the dice with a passion.

JEAN
Yes it was, I'm telling you . . . believe me.

MATHIEU
(*lights a cigarette*)
No it wasn't. I'll stake my life on it!

JEAN
You don't remember, listen . . .

MATHIEU
Who, me?

JEAN
Listen, old man, it was his wife, after all!

MATHIEU
So?

JEAN
He had to be with her regardless in a situation like that, didn't he?

MATHIEU

Granted, but he couldn't have gone missing, couldn't have abandoned his post for that length of time. His post at the station. Think about it for just one second!

I'm serving a very lively table, at which Marc and Thomas are sitting, among others. I feel Thomas's hand touch my thigh. The hand moves higher. But it is hesitant, content merely to brush my skin. It tickles . . . I carry on pouring wine into glasses that are straightaway emptied by the drinkers. I can't stand it anymore! I take a step backward to rid myself of the fumbling hand. I spill wine everywhere: over the table, on Marc's trousers.

"What's got into you?"

"He was tickling me!"

I look behind me, at the camera. I feel like bursting into laughter. I don't drop the bottle, but it's tilted: the wine pours out, all over the place. Marc stands up, losing his temper, he doesn't understand what's going on, wine has spilled even on his shoes. He jerks his arms, yells something, tries to protect himself by climbing up on his chair. The cameraman and the director are doubled up with laughter. Thomas smiles, looking at his hands. The others come closer, out of curiosity.

"What's going on? What happened?"

"Nothing serious," says the director. And he bursts out laughing. "We'll do another take."

Standing on his chair, Marc bursts out laughing too. Everybody is having fun. The director rubs his hands together.

"The atmosphere is perfect! Let's do another take. Go behind the bar with Jean. No, wait! How did it go? Ah, yes. Jean was talking to Mathieu. That's right. The station-master was playing dice. With the peasants. Great. You'll do all that again for me. Focus an arc light on the bar!"

Everybody is talking at the same time. Somebody goes and puts a coin in the jukebox. Music!

"I need to go and get changed," says Marc, still perched on top of his chair.

"No need. Let's get on with it! No time to waste!"

But the cameraman wants to have a word in the director's ear. For example:

"You want an arc light on the countertop. Isn't that a bit much?"

"Not at all."

"It's not needed, let me assure you . . ."

"Yes, it is."

"All right, have it your own way . . . But I'm adding a dimmer."

"To your places, everybody! Where's the clapper board? Quiet on the set!"

He's so excited that I don't dare complain about Thomas's fumbling. Or rather about his lack of conviction. And since he didn't demand an explanation . . . He didn't demand anything. And I don't have the time to tell him either. I don't say anything. I decide to keep myself more under control. Here's what I need to do: I rub very hard up against Thomas's knee. That works! Now he's more certain of himself. He's really feeling me up now, the lecher! There's a look of concentration on his face. His fingers touch my knickers, move higher, rub my labia, my clitoris. It's nice. But I draw back a little. I'm trying to overhear the conversation on the other side.

MATHIEU
It was during the war. Think about it for a moment!

JEAN
No it wasn't. Don't exaggerate. The war was over by
then.

MATHIEU
Over?

JEAN
Yes, over. Or do you think it's still going on?

Now that I've finished pouring wine into the glasses—
they're being emptied at a slower rate—it's time for me to
get back behind the bar. I move out of the frame, or at
least I hope I do, because I'm standing next to the boom
operator. Are they doing a different take already? I can't see
the camera anymore. The director is shouting out words
that are unintelligible. What language is he speaking? The
boom operator looks like he's having a whale of a time. He
turns to me, he is about to say something, but it's not the
right moment . . . I crouch down to discourage him. "It's
just a rehearsal," he says. I close my eyes to avoid the glare
of a spotlight on the bar, which somebody has forgotten
to turn off.

FIRST PEASANT
Double six. Got you!

SECOND PEASANT
Drat!

"Cut!" yells the director, so loudly that everybody jumps.

What's got into him? We're not filming . . .

"Where's Marie? For God's sake! Where is she?"

I'm huddled behind the bar, with the script on my knees. He comes up to me, furious.

"What the hell are you doing back here?"

I stand up, without making any reply. I attempt a smile. I show him the burgundy folder. I find it a horrible color . . .

"Give it here!"

I hand him the script. He snatches it from me, opens it, finally finds the right page. He reads aloud, as if reciting:

"Marie lets all the men in the bistro feel her up. She's maternal in her gestures. Are you listening to me?"

"I'm not deaf!"

"Here she is stroking a peasant's unruly mop of hair. Aroused, the peasant stands up. The booze distorts his voice:

'"PEASANT
'"Mathieu, how about you sing a song?

'"THOMAS
'"He's right. Give us a song!'

"Now do you understand?"

I merely nod.

"Come here. We'll do it all over again. Everybody ready?"

I go back to the same table, holding a fresh bottle.

Thomas continues his rummaging under my skirt. More and more insistently. More and more effectively . . .

A VOICE
Sing, Mathieu! Sing!

A VOICE
Give us a song!

A VOICE
Sing!

Mathieu reluctantly agrees. He would rather have continued his conversation with Jean. He stubs out his cigarette in an ashtray.

MATHIEU
You're wrong there. It was during the war . . .

JEAN
(*conciliatorily*)
All right, whatever you say. But now you'd better sing!

Mathieu sings. He hams it up all the way. He has the body language of a 1940s crooner. But the people in the bistro love it. They tap the tables in time to the song. Jean does a few dance moves. Everybody is in high spirits. Everybody is happy. Except perhaps Marc. He's probably noticed what Thomas is up to and doesn't seem to take kindly to it. He looks at the red stain on his light gray trousers. At his shoes, which are now burgundy. There's a break in the filming. But Thomas can't tear himself away from my thigh. He stares at me, with questioning eyes. I feel hot.

He makes an effort and withdraws his hand. They turn the spotlights off. Ugh! I'm all wet. The lighting technician hands me a drink. I think it's the lighting technician. There are a lot of people. It's too hot. Sweaty, excited faces. Radiant faces, in fact. I unbutton my shirt lower. The director is going back and forth. He congratulates me.

"That blouse suits you really well."

"It's not a blouse."

His eyes travel over my breasts. Behind him, Thomas is studying his hands. He would do well to file his nails.

We're all thirsty. We drink.

Marc is about to vanish somewhere.

I find myself standing really close to Jean C. He has been sitting all the while, calmly, cupping the dice in his hand. He gestures to me. I don't know what he means by that. I lean over, place my ear next to his mouth, which utters words that are inaudible. Everybody is talking very loudly. The director starts bawling, his face scarlet. He takes himself a little bit too seriously.

"You shouldn't take it too . . ."

Was it Jean who said that? I feel a hard, metal object poking my behind. Like the barrel of a gun. The cameraman apologizes: it was because somebody else pushed him.

"It's like a war zone," he says, with a toothy grin. He must have been saving up that remark for quite a while. He delivers it in a satisfied tone of voice.

"Never mind . . ."

He's handsome, but a little daft.

I ask Jean whether he's happy. He shrugs, mutters:

"What a mess."

"Everybody back to work!"

The man is out of his mind! I shout back at him:

"I need to go and get changed!"

He doesn't seem to have heard me. He keeps shouting:

"Everybody back to work!"

I shout back at him again:

"I need to get changed!"

"Just go," mutters Jean C. and casts the dice.

I go behind the bar, where I've left the script, and then head for the stairs. I go upstairs. I can still hear the increasingly strangulated voice of the director as he shouts for everybody to get back to work. Marc is sitting on the step at the top of the stairs, in the shadows. Is he crying or lurking?

"What's up with you?"

I look closely at his face. He isn't crying. On the contrary, he's laughing. Or almost. He seems amused. He strokes my leg, above the knee. He doesn't get any higher.

"Let me get past."

He doesn't say anything. He goes on stroking my leg. But he does so in a consoling or even encouraging way.

Back in my room, I lie down on the bed. I'm sick of it all. I'm knackered. As if to justify my lying here, I open the script. How asinine the dialogue is! True, I'm not keen on so-called witty dialogue, but even so, you can take it too far in the opposite direction . . . Just listen to this:

SCENE 19. INT. THE BISTRO

Mathieu stops singing. He can't go on forever. He lifts his hand to his throat.

MATHIEU
I can't go on!

A VOICE
Sing another!

A VOICE
Encore!

A VOICE
Be nice to us!

Imperturbable, the stationmaster casts the dice.

MATHIEU
No, I've had enough. And besides, I don't have any
musical backing . . .

THOMAS
We'll put some music on!

He gets up to put a coin in the jukebox. Music. Mathieu
starts singing again. This time his voice has an orchestral
accompaniment. Which is to say, he is forced to impro-
vise against the musical background. He even stops to ask
for a light. But that doesn't matter. Everybody is happy.
Probably it's not the first time he's resorted to such a ruse.
    "Marie!"
    "Is that you, Jean?"
    "Yes, it's me . . ."
Jean C. pokes his head around the half-open door.

"Come downstairs, you're needed . . ."

"I'll be there in five minutes. Come in, if you like."

He slips inside the room without closing the door. He seems troubled and conspiratorial at the same time. He looks for something in his waistcoat pocket. He takes out a photograph.

"What's that?"

He hands me the photo without a word. A photo of Marc, in military uniform. Standing with a rifle in his hand.

"Is that Marc?"

He nods his head up and down like an old woman.

"And?"

"He looks good in uniform."

It's true, he does look good. He looks very young. Behind him, you can make out a forest.

I put on a bra and change my shirt. J. C. has put the photograph back in his pocket and is looking out of the window.

"Are we still rehearsing or are we filming now?"

He doesn't know. We'll go downstairs and see.

Downstairs, in the bistro, the din is deafening. The director is trying to make himself heard above everybody else.

"I'm sick of the whole lot of you! Everybody back to work!"

WITH HIS EYES fixed on the stairs, Jean calls to Marie.

The only people at the cutting room table are Marie-Jeanne and the director, who looks weary. The same as he does every evening.

Jean's voice:

"Marie!"

In Marc's room, Marie looks out of the window. On the wall, level with her head, there is a poster showing a lion hunt. At the edge of a forest. The lion is too yellow. It looks like a lemon smeared with mustard. The scene needs to be cut. Or given less emphasis. There should be a greater emphasis on the four men carrying the stretcher. But not too much, let's not go over the top . . .

Jean's voice:

"Marie!"

Mathieu stops singing, takes offence.

"What's got into you?"

Two voices of protest:

"Let him sing, you chucklehead!"

"I'm not singing anymore."

Mathieu goes to the bar and orders a beer.

The stationmaster is playing dice. He shakes the dice in his fist for a long while before throwing them.

"Double six!"

"What luck!"

Jean is talking to Mathieu.

"If we hadn't transported her by stretcher . . ."

"That's true, very true . . ."

And then another five takes of the same scene. The last two of which are botched: Mathieu fluffed his lines and there wasn't enough light.

"Turn on the other spotlight," somebody shouted.

"Cut!"

The clapper board yet again.

"Quiet on the set!"

Marie-Jeanne's eyes are sore. She presses a button, the small screen turns white, a dirty white, but it's soothing even so. Near her, a voice murmurs, the voice of somebody who has just woken up with a start:

"What are you doing?"

"My eyes are aching."

She lifts her glasses and rubs her eyes with the back of her hand. After a few seconds, she says, as if by way of an explanation:

"Which one are we going to keep? Make your mind up."

The man makes no reply. He gropes for the film editor's hand, doesn't find it.

"Where are you?"

"I'm here."

She is standing up, two paces away. He still can't see her.

"Turn on the light!"

"What?"

"I said turn on the light if you're tired."

"I'm not tired. My eyes are sore."

"Same difference."

He looks for his lighter, doesn't find it. The film editor

sits back down and, with her left hand, feels the buttons, presses one, goes to the wrong place, rewinds.

Jean's voice:

"Marie!"

Marie-Jeanne presses fast-forward.

"I can't find my lighter."

She pauses on an image of a forest glade or a meadow above the forest, where we see the terrace of a large sanatorium: patients recumbent on chaises longues, blond nurses going back and forth among them, a parrot in a cage. She hands the director a lighter. All we can hear is the jumbled sound of conversations in German. "Thanks." He hands her back the lighter. She cannot refrain from asking:

"What's with this scene?"

"I spliced it together. Along with a few others."

"You're getting carried away. What's the point of my being here, in that case?"

A soaring eagle and Marc's voice, off camera:

"Get him to shut his beak!"

"Stop!" says the director.

But by now we're seeing a different image: the stationmaster on the platform, waving his flag. He gazes in the direction of the forest. Motionless. The film editor's eyes are really aching. She takes off her glasses. Sitting next to her, the director is silent. He is staring at the image of the stationmaster on the platform and seems utterly fascinated. Or maybe he too is contemplating the forest . . .

"My eyes are aching. I'm going outside to smoke a cigarette."

Marie-Jeanne finally strikes the right tone, just in time. The director doesn't say anything. He can't be bothered to reply. He hears the door close behind her.

On the screen, we now see the outline of Marie, who is looking out of the window. On the floor is a television: a path through the forest. Rustling leaves, birdsong. Marie turns around, stoops to turn the sound off. She sits down next to Marc on the bed. She strokes his forehead, his hair. Four men are carrying a stretcher. The image expands and then vanishes. Marie goes downstairs to the bistro, where people are talking noisily. She goes behind the bar.

"Has the wine in this dive run out or what?"

Before the bar customer can finish saying his line off camera, Marie bursts out laughing. And yet again Marie comes downstairs, but she stumbles, loses a shoe, falls to her knees. The bar customer repeats the line about the wine running out, Marie doesn't burst out laughing this time, but in the end the first take was still better. How could she not burst out laughing? She's full of merriment, that Marie!

Now she steps back into the frame, holding a fat bottle, and starts pouring. Every hand touches her. She lets herself be felt up and at intervals she laughs: as if it tickled.

The switchman is talking to a peasant who is cradling a lamb.

"How many did you say?"

"Well, er . . . four. One on each side."

"Bugger it!"

"What's wrong?"

"The filthy animal just pissed on me!"

"Cut!"

He puts the lamb down. It bleats.

The clapper board. At the bar, Jean is talking to Mathieu.

"You can believe me, Mathieu, I'm telling you it was after the war. Remember, the stretcher . . ."

"Ah, but it's the other woman you're talking about! In that case, we're a green . . . Sorry!"

"Cut!"

"Clapper board!"

"Action!"

"We're a greedy . . ."

"Cut!"

"Clapper board!"

"Action!"

"We're agreed! We're completely agreed!"

But Jean is not listening anymore. He's looking at Marc, who's down on all fours, playing the wolf.

"Look at that idiot," says Jean.

"Cut!"

And in the next shot, the lamb takes fright and bolts. Marc chases it, still on all fours.

"What a moron," thinks the director and promises himself that he will redo all the shots tomorrow.

Marc and the lamb are now behind the bar with Marie. They are out of sight. Nobody takes any more notice of them. Not even the director, who is still at the cutting room table, his eyes closed, breathing steadily, as if he were asleep.

I GO DOWNSTAIRS. In the bistro, everybody is growing more and more animated: they drink, chatter, play dice, shout, sing. A real shindig. I hesitate, come to a stop. I see the director. He's signaling to me, but I don't know what he means: should I continue coming down the stairs or isn't it my turn yet? He then shouts:

"Let's do another take!"

They set up the camera in the doorway that gives onto the square. But I can see another one that seems to be pointed at the bar. So, now they're playing a duet.

I go behind the bar, where I've stashed another copy of the script.

A VOICE
Has the wine run out in this dive or what?

All right, now it's my turn. I pick up a bottle and start pouring. I go from one table to another and let myself be felt up: they slap my buttocks, pinch my thighs. Nothing nastier than that. It's a good-natured ritual, and I have to laugh it off. I have to laugh. Like everybody else.

The switchman talks to a peasant who is cradling a lamb. But I can't see the boom operator. This must be a rehearsal. Yet another one!

Marc is down on all fours, howling like a wolf. The director isn't satisfied. He too gets down on all fours.

"Not like that," he says. And he starts roaring.

"Am I pretending to be a wolf or a lion?" asks Marc.

"Both."

Obviously, given all this, the lamb takes fright. It bolts. Marc chases after it, still on all fours.

"Action!" shouts the director.

But it's too late: Marc and the lamb are now behind the bar, out of sight.

There ensues a brief discussion between the director and the cameraman, who doesn't seem to appreciate the director's method of working.

"If you really wanted to capture that," he says, "you should have warned me in advance."

"I couldn't have predicted that would happen."

"Yeah, right . . ."

The cameraman's voice is scornful. But the director is so forlorn and disappointed that the cameraman's scorn finally dissolves into tenderness.

"All right, we'll do another take," says the cameraman.

But no, now the director has come up with a different idea.

"We'll film behind the bar."

The cameraman shrugs and doesn't say anything more. He sets up the camera on a box in the doorway of the toilet.

"Mind you don't fall backward down the bog!" shouts the boom operator.

The cameraman storms out of the toilet.

"It stinks in there!"

"It doesn't matter. You're not filming the smell."

"Flush it . . ."

"Let me see what's what," says the director in the firm voice of a general who doesn't hesitate to put himself on the front line. It's true: it stinks in there! He pulls the chain. "Somebody had a shit and missed the bowl," he announces and comes back out, stamping his feet.

"Everybody in position!" he shouts. He now has a megaphone, which he waves about at the drop of a hat.

"Marc, Marie, behind the bar. With the lamb!"

But where is the lamb?

They look everywhere but can't find it. Maybe it's sneaked outside.

"We can't film without the lamb," says the continuity girl, waving her notebook.

Luckily, one of the other peasants has another lamb. Albeit a larger one, almost sheep-sized.

"That's a sheep," says the continuity girl, outraged.

"I beg your pardon, miss, but this isn't a sheep. It's just a bit sturdy, that's all," says the peasant, offering his animal for the glory of the seventh art.

"It's not the same one."

The continuity girl is adamant. Not even the director is able to make her budge.

"We're only rehearsing," he says.

"But it's too big!"

Meanwhile, a team led by Jean C. leaves the bistro in search of the original lamb. They proceed to the square and come to a halt at the spot where the monument ought to be. It would seem that J. C. cannot help but broach the subject of the missing monument yet again. He raises his arm, pointing with his index finger. Or his fist.

"Everybody in position!" repeats the director. Although in the circumstances the order makes no sense.

"Are we rehearsing?"

"Yes, we are. We'll rehearse with the sheep until we find the lamb."

Behind the bar, Marc is playing with the sheep next to my feet. I clap and ask Mathieu to sing.

"What's got into you?" says the director.

"What do you mean what's got into me? I'm clapping. I'm doing what it says in the script."

But Mathieu is unable to sing. For the simple reason that he is outside, looking for the lamb. But fortunately, the accordionist is still here to create a little atmosphere, so that they actors won't seem too wooden.

Marc is now playing with my legs rather than with the sheep. Sticking rigidly to the script, I let him have his way. And the director is happy, even if Marc isn't here to sing or encourage the accordionist, who nonetheless plays with gusto. All by himself.

Everybody is drinking heavily. They're going to get blotto.

The peasant has come behind the bar, looking for his lamb—or his sheep, if you prefer—which has taken refuge next to Jean.

Finally, the scouts return with a lamb. But it's too small . . .

"That's not the same one either," says the continuity girl, almost bursting into tears. "It's too small . . ."

"Never mind, it'll do! I'm the one who has the final say on what size it should be," shouts the director into his megaphone.

Jeanne-Marie, the continuity girl, looks at him in despair and wonders whether or not she should hand in her resignation.

Mathieu starts singing before the clapper board comes down. It's a different song, one the accordionist isn't all that familiar with. He has difficulty playing the accompaniment.

"Action!"

Marc and the peasant both caress my calves and then my thighs. And I have to pretend to be interested only in the music . . .

Another peasant, probably sozzled, drops a glass.

Night has fallen and we're still filming. Another scene. There's no longer any need to rehearse. By now the bistro is a real madhouse. Everybody is drunk to a greater or lesser degree, apart from the accordionist, who plays with great delight. Behind the bar, Jean has dozed off. The stationmaster isn't here. He must be at the station. At a table, Thomas and Mathieu are busy drinking. There are some peonies in an earthenware pot: the most sensuous of all perfumes.

"Action!"

They're all drinking like there's no tomorrow. The actors are identifying more and more with their characters. Each is giving it his all. I sit down on a chair. Half-naked as I am, I feel a little cold. Marc is slumped on the floor next to me, resting his head in my lap. A peasant is doing his utmost to unfasten my bra.

"Don't be in such a hurry," says the director, chiding him.

And I have to put my bra back on for the sixth time.

"We're rolling!"

This time, the peasant can't unfasten it and loses his temper. I laugh. I can't remember whether I have to laugh, but I don't care: I feel like it and so I roar with laughter.

MARIE
Need a hand?

Thomas is still talking to Mathieu.

THOMAS
What about at night?

MATHIEU
At night?

THOMAS
Yes. At night. Did you stop?

MATHIEU
Not at all. Only if necessary . . . what I mean is, only if night fell before we got there . . . But then we would carry on, obviously. By torchlight. You see?

The peasant finally manages it. I congratulate him, kiss him on the mouth.

MARIE
Bravo, darling!

It's the peasant with the lamb. He's called François.

FRANÇOIS
I deserve more than just a kiss!

MARIE
Don't push your luck . . .

Another glass breaks. The accordionist has run out of steam. Marc is asleep, his head resting on my thighs. Sitting all by himself at a table, off camera, the director is reluctant to shout: "Cut!"

LYING IN BED with my eyes wide open, I'm probably waiting for the alarm clock to ring. I look all around the room. Am I uneasy? When the alarm clock rings, I jump out of bed. I'm wearing long johns and an undervest. I start to do some exercises, or rather, I swing my arms a few times. I stop. I go over to the window: the sun is shining on the small square, which still lacks a monument. The station is in the distance. And farther still, the hills.

I go to the washbasin. I haven't shaved for a few days.

The script is on the table, in the place of honor. I pull on my trousers, put on my waistcoat. My uniform, in other words. I read the script standing up.

The stationmaster is no longer looking out of the window. He looks undecided; he doesn't exactly know what to do. He seems to be waiting for something. As ever.

He goes to the washbasin, looks in the mirror. He grimaces, then smiles. He needs to have a shave. He shrugs. He begins to get dressed. He's in more and more of a hurry. He walks a few paces around the room, shuffling his boots. His every movement recalls the first scenes of the film. But nota bene! The photograph of the woman is to be found only in the first scene.

He goes to the cupboard and takes out an album, which he flicks through. We glimpse photographs and postcards:

Jean behind the bar;

a peasant cradling a lamb;

Mathieu singing;

an eagle in flight, with a big fish in its claws;

Marc dancing with Marie (this photograph is blurred);

a huge snake about to lunge at a rabbit;

a train carriage packed with soldiers;

Mathieu and Thomas at the edge of a forest;

Marc again, as a private in the army;

a lion hunt (in Africa?);

Marie at the station, in front of the clump of peonies and the rosebushes;

a blue, yellow, and red toucan in a cage . . .

The door opens to reveal Marc's hirsute face. He doesn't enter the room but merely sticks his head inside and chuckles:

"How's it going, Dad?"

The face then disappears and the door slams shut behind it.

I don't get annoyed. Without making haste, I go to the door. I open it and look down the corridor. Marc is standing with his ear pressed to another door.

"What are you up to over there?"

He makes no reply. He glances at me and then carries on eavesdropping. The sound of rustling leaves and then, more loudly, as if in the foreground, groans of an erotic variety. What he's doing isn't at all acceptable . . . I return to my room, grab the burgundy folder, go back out. He's still there, the bastard! Crouching with his ear pressed to the keyhole, he's eavesdropping. In this particular case, one can hardly talk about voyeurism, because he can't see anything. What he can now see are my shoes and the bottoms of my trousers. I tap his shoulder.

"Stand up!"

But he doesn't budge. He doesn't seem embarrassed. Not one bit. I'm starting to get annoyed. I don't really know what attitude to take. I don't say anything. I don't budge. Now I'm listening too. I turn one ear toward the door. But there's nothing more to be heard. Except the distant sound of voices, but that's coming from elsewhere, from the bistro downstairs.

"What are you hanging around here for? Back to work, you idler!"

I go downstairs, with the script tucked under my arm.

Behind the bar, Jean is in a good mood. He's humming the tune to one of the songs Mathieu sang yesterday. A little later, the stationmaster and the switchman sit down at a table to have breakfast.

MARC
I'd like another coffee. And some milk . . .

JEAN
Coming right up.

MARC
And some sausage . . .

Jean makes the coffee, slices some sausage. As he is bringing over the tray, he puts a foot wrong and almost falls over. The cup of coffee spills all over the tray. He returns behind the bar, exclaiming: "I'm back!" He pours another cup of coffee. Adds the milk.

JEAN
You're as hungry as a wolf, you are!

MARC
(*like a spoiled child*)
I'm hungry, I'm hungry . . .

STATIONMASTER
(*irritated*)
Cut it out!

MARC
I'm as hungry as a lion!

Marc starts pulling faces, but the stationmaster doesn't pay any attention to him. He serenely drinks his coffee, his thoughts apparently elsewhere.

JEAN
(*prodding his head with one finger*)
Screw loose?

The bearded man giggles inanely and fidgets in his seat: he wriggles his legs like a small child displaying delight or impatience.
Mathieu comes down the stairs, humming the same tune as Jean just now. He is holding a cigarette between his thumb and index finger.

MATHIEU
How's it going, everybody?

MARC
Fine, fine. I'm hungry . . .

Mathieu goes over to the bar.

JEAN
What are you having?

MATHIEU
Coffee and a cognac. For starters . . .

He laughs. Jean laughs too, and starts making the coffee.

JEAN
Listen, Mathieu, you were right yesterday. It was before the war. You were right.

MATHIEU
(*highly satisfied*)
There, you see?
(*He falls silent for a few seconds, staring at his coffee cup, and then continues*)
But it depends . . .

JEAN
(*astonished*)
What do you mean, it depends?

MATHIEU
Of course it does!
(*lowers his voice*)

It's all to do with his wife, with Marie or . . . But forget about it for now. We'll talk about it later. Understand?

Jean makes a gesture to show he understands.

A little after that, the stationmaster stands up, ready to go back to the station. The flag is in his pocket.

STATIONMASTER
(*to Marc*)
Aren't you coming?

MARC
Yes, but I haven't finished!

The stationmaster shrugs and goes outside.

The stationmaster makes his entrance. His face is puffy, he has dark rings under his eyes, like somebody who hasn't slept well or hasn't slept at all. He moves his lips by way of a greeting and sits down opposite me. With his fingertips he touches the page of the script that lies open in front of me, clears his throat, pulls out a handkerchief to dislodge a buildup of mucus. All this with the praiseworthy intention of regaining his voice and being able to articulate some small phrase expressing his satisfaction at seeing, so early in the morning, the actors at work, with the pages of the script spread in front of them, at seeing them preparing for a fresh day of filming, conscientiously learning even the least significant lines, but in vain: he coughs, hawks, blows his nose, clears his throat, points a finger at the script, gets annoyed, chokes, gasps for air, bangs his fist on the table, causing the cup of coffee he has just been brought to spill all over the typewritten pages. He just can't manage it: guttural noises issue from his mouth, and his gestures become increasingly violent, increasingly expressive.

He spent almost the whole of yesterday looking at the dailies sent to him by the lab, which developed them in record time. He invited the actors to attend too, but only Jean C. is here: he watches impassively, without comment, and seemingly without moving a muscle. Nevertheless, he is not perfectly motionless, and a novelist with a fine sense of observation, one of those novelists who delight the public with their omniscience and even their omnipresence, would note that at intervals our actor takes a small bottle from his pocket, raising it to his lips with precision. This explains why, having arrived quite late, rather than sitting down next to the director, he preferred to keep his distance. And when the director suggested he move closer, he merely made a friendly but firm gesture which, in spoken language, might signify: It's all right, old man, I'm fine where I am.

"But you can't see from over there," says the director, shifting restlessly in his chair.

And J. C. repeats the same gesture: He raises both hands to eye level, with the palms turned toward the director, and slightly inclines his head toward his left shoulder.

The director insists:

"Come over here!"

"I've got good eyesight," says J. C. defensively, mimicking the voice of Jean Gabin.

On the screen we see the little station, the forest, the wooded hills. A troop train passes without stopping. On the platform, the stationmaster lowers his flag. To his right, he sees Marc, who is sweeping aimlessly. Noticing that he is under observation, he begins to sweep more quickly, making jerky movements. It ought to be funny. But it isn't really.

The stationmaster walks up to him. The bearded man retreats, still sweeping. He shuffles his feet like Charlie Chaplin.

"He's laying it on a bit thick," says the director.

The stationmaster looks over to the telegraph office. He goes up to the door, opens it: nobody there. Marc takes the opportunity to scarper.

The stationmaster comes back, takes note that the switchman has disappeared, shakes his head. He ought to look indulgent or even amused. The director pauses on this frame and examines it for a few seconds, long enough to ascertain that the stationmaster sooner looks disconsolate.

"What do you think of that?"

The question comes just as J. C. has raised the bottle to his lips. He quickly lowers it, chokes, coughs, clears his throat, but doesn't know what to reply. He says, "Well, yeah, it's okay . . ."

"It's not okay at all," says the director and turns his head just as the actor is putting the bottle back in his pocket. It's not funny!

"Not really," agrees the actor in a faint voice.

"What are you up to over there?"

"Nothing . . ."

"Come over here, next to me! Over here, on my right. We'll watch it together," says the director in an imperious voice. Browbeaten, the actor can no longer refuse, he complies: he gets up, still fiddling with the bottle in his pocket, goes over to the director, and slowly sits down.

"Are you still asleep or what?"

"No, quite the opposite," answers Jean C. and decides to show him the bottle.

"Ah, so that's it! That changes everything," exclaims the director. "Give it here!"

The director grabs the bottle, raises it to his lips . . .

"Damned stopper!"

J. C. watches him. He shakes his head, looking indulgent, even amused.

"Good, is it?"

"Not bad." The director clicks his tongue. He puts the bottle of calvados on the editing table, next to the screen.

"I meant the film."

"Oh, the film . . ."

Brought back to reality, the director studies the paused frame: the stationmaster in close-up, with a smile that is more like a rictus. The director says:

"No, this needs to be cut. We can't end on a close-up."

The actor nods in agreement and reaches to take the bottle.

"What are you doing?"

"The bottle . . ."

"The bottle, all very well, but this needs to be cut . . ."

"I don't know anything about that kind of thing," says J. C. He raises the bottle to his lips. He does so as if in slow motion, which seems to annoy the director.

"You don't know anything about that kind of thing . . . You don't even know how to smile! I'm not saying I don't like that gob of yours, as baleful as the lips of a carp lurking in the depths, but even so, you ought to smile every now and then. And when a smile is required, then smile, for God's sake! As Godard said . . ."

"Who? Oh, you mean the . . ."

On the screen, the stationmaster is still motionless. His rictus is blatant. He can't have been feeling well. Maybe he had a bellyache.

"Pass me the bottle."

J. C. hesitates before handing him the receptacle.

"But it's empty . . . You quaffed the lot!" cries the director, giving the bottle a shake. "Unbelievable!" His voice becomes more and more admiring. "You're jam-packed with booze! But even so, you never get pissed. Whereas I was completely slaughtered yesterday, you saw me yourself . . . I reached the point where I couldn't even talk."

"No big deal . . ."

"What do you mean, no big deal? You're just saying it . . . But how do you do it? What's your secret?"

Jean C. realizes that the director can't help talking crap. There's nothing that can be done about it. He says slowly:

"Don't take it to heart . . ."

"I'm not taking it to heart, for God's sake! I admire you and I declare my admiration loud and clear."

"All right, but declare it a little less loudly. Everybody will think we're having an argument."

"I couldn't care less if they do . . ."

He finally calms down. He looks at the image on the screen: the stationmaster in close-up, his sour smile, his two eyes.

"Maybe you're right. So what, anyway!"

He presses a button and the stationmaster's face vanishes

as if by magic, immediately to be replaced by Marie's bottom, her fat bottom. Before an open window.

In bed, the telegraph operator stirs beneath the blanket. He snorts with impatience.

"Are you coming?"

Marie looks out of the window at the small square, which still lacks a monument. By now it's too late. Even if the monument were to be delivered, there would be nothing they could do with it now. It's too late. It's raining, a summer shower. It will soon stop. Marie sees the stationmaster walking toward the bistro. She watches, calm and smiling. At least she knows how to smile!

"Are you coming?"

Marie contemplates the stationmaster's stiff-legged gait and waits for him to leave the frame. Only then does she traverse the three or four paces that lie between her and the bed.

"Coming!"

In the corridor, Marc is listening, with his ear pressed to a door.

And then, in the bistro, all three of them, Mathieu, Jean, and Marie, sit at a table, just about to finish their breakfast. Mathieu asks for a coffee. He smacks his lips and says:

"Exquisite. You're now going to fix us some coffee, aren't you?"

"Of course."

Marie stands up and goes behind the bar. She discovers a lamb huddled in the corner.

"Look, a lamb!" She puts her arms around it and strokes it. "How cute it is!"

"They must have left it here last night."

"Poor thing!"

"Give it something to eat and drink," suggests Mathieu.

Marie sees to the lamb. She gives it some milk. She's very motherly. Naturally!

Thomas comes down the stairs. At full speed.

And the train enters the station. A few peasants alight. The stationmaster walks with Thomas to the steps of a carriage. He is talking, tugging the telegraph operator by the sleeve, in fact, no, that's trite, the director smiles and turns his head toward J. C., who, holding the empty calvados bottle, sits impassively.

"It's still got some air in it!"

The director is delighted at his own wit.

On the screen, the stationmaster playfully tugs the telegraph operator's necktie but pulls too hard.

"Ow, that hurts!"

The director starts to laugh. All by himself. The actor remains stony-faced. He has no inclination to smile. He'd like to get out of there. He's racking his brains to come up with an excuse to leave.

The stationmaster walks with Thomas to the steps of a carriage. He grasps him by the arm, comes to a halt, looks down at the telegraph operator's shoes, and then, without haste, slowly raises his head until he is looking his young interlocutor in the eye.

"You'll tell them everything that's necessary. Got that?"

"Got it, boss!"

"And don't forget the frock. I want it to be really pretty. I'm relying on you."

"Got it, boss. I've got a knack . . ."

The stationmaster walks a few yards away and raises his flag. The train sets in motion.

"I need to take a piss," says J. C.

At the window of a carriage, two soldiers are laughing and joking. At another window sits a young woman who looks like Marie. But we can't be sure, because the train is picking up speed.

"I'm going out to take a piss," says J. C. and slowly stands up, still holding the bottle. But the director isn't listening.

The train picks up speed and J. C. really does need to take a piss. He hurries to the door. Oh well! The station-master shrugs, and so does the director. He looks at the vacant chair on his right. He turns his head, hears the door close, and goes back to looking at the screen, where the stationmaster has also just closed a door: the door to the telegraph office. All these noises need to be superimposed on the soundtrack to the next scene. The director rubs his hands together.

Is he satisfied? Is he thinking about the next day's filming? It's going to be one of the key scenes of the film, a long scene consisting of outdoor shots, which will pose quite a few lighting difficulties.

The weather will be fine tomorrow, decides the director, and deep in thought, he forgets to turn off the now blank screen.

It's BETTER WRITTEN than the screenplay, better translated, that is. I turn back to the first page to check: sure enough, there's the translator's name, black on white.

> *... Slightly flexing her knees, she spread her long arms and flapped them like wings, before abruptly moving them in front of her and using her hands to indicate some object very small in size, whereupon she spread her arms once more and waved them up and down a few times. She's a loony, the stationmaster said to himself, and gently stroked his chin. Maybe you're hungry, he said, raising two fingers to his lips, and then placed his hand over his stomach, but she continued to flap her arms and, at intervals, leaned toward him and indicated some kind of small object with her hands: a cup, or a snake, or a parrot, he couldn't tell what. She then took him by the hand and pulled him toward the train. As they climbed the steps of the carriage he admired her legs and her haunches, clad in tight blue trousers, he followed her down the corridor, they entered a compartment, she turned to him and smiled.*

I hear the director's voice calling us. Already? I close the book, take a final swig of coffee, and head for the back door. I open it and am dazzled by the light. The sun is blazing. So too the grass: the thousand-watt bulbs and arc lights are at full blast, pouring out their raw, pitiless glare. The electricians are bustling around these monstrous eyes, whose frozen rage envelops the field all the way into the distance. The few animals that are about, cows and sheep, are no longer grazing; it's as if they're being roasted, while the chirping of the birds is louder than usual.

Cradling a lamb, the director yells, flings out orders. He's talking to a bald man, the director of photography. The director raises his arms, still holding the lamb, and the bald man holds out his arms to receive it, in fact no, the director's body language is confusing: he merely wanted to point out a cloud that has drifted above the hills and which looks like a gigantic ewe.

"We need to be quick!"

"Don't worry, the wind is blowing in the other direction."

"There you go again with the direction . . ."

"What?"

"Are you sure? About the direction . . ."

"Absolutely sure!"

Another voice calls to me: "Come over here, if you please!" The makeup artist is in a hurry too. She has long blond hair tied in two pigtails. Everybody says we look alike. But I find her a tad skinny. As well as annoying, what with the "if you please" she tacks on to the end of every sentence. So much so that everybody calls her Marie If You Please. But she couldn't care less; she just smiles, baring her overly long canines.

Seated at a table, Jean and Mathieu are drinking red wine. They wave to me and wink conspiratorially.

"Come and have a drink with us."

"It's better inside . . ."

"It's quieter."

Marc, assisted by a grip, carries a table outside and then some chairs. They put them down on the grass, following the instructions of the director, who, armed with his trusty megaphone, keeps changing his mind about where. The door is open and the bistro is lit up like the stage of a theater.

"Come over here!"

"It's very nice over here."

In the same instant, the front door opens and François enters the bistro.

"Hello, everybody!"

"Hello, François."

"How's it going?"

Glass in hand, Mathieu nods and drinks. Jean stands up.

"Are you having a drink?"

The peasant doesn't have time to reply. The director runs inside and shouts:

"Everybody outside!"

And then he runs back out again.

"What's going on?"

"Not a lot, says Jean. We're going to have a drink outside. We're going to be filming, I mean."

He grabs the bottle, the two glasses, and looks at Mathieu, who is not at all convinced that there is any need for this sudden change of scene or for all the commotion the director is making.

"The place isn't on fire . . ."

He stubs out his cigarette, but doesn't budge from

where he is sitting. Jean and François go outside, laden with glasses and bottles. The makeup artist hands me a mirror and says:

"Who is the fairest?"

I find her jolliness rather forced, but it gives Mathieu a good excuse to heave himself to his feet and start walking. His limbs are heavy, his back bent. He comes to a halt in front of us and sticks his thumb up.

"Top notch!"

He's looking not at me, but at Marie If You Please. She blushes.

Jean and François come back in, with two grips or electricians, in search of more chairs. The director's megaphone booms:

"Everybody outside!"

Mathieu finally makes his mind up. He sticks his tobacco-stained thumb up once more and heads toward the exit, taking short steps. We all go outside. I'm blinded by the combined glare of the sun and the spotlights. I raise my arm to shield my eyes.

The lamb is on the table, among the glasses and bottles. It must be frightened, but at the same time it must be paralyzed by the floods of light enveloping it, since it remains standing, dignified, without flinching. All around it, the crystal glasses glitter and add to the dazzle of the scene.

"Look, Marie!"

"I see it. We're going to get slaughtered yet again."

In silence, everybody looks at the lamb and listens to the quavering voice of the director as he utters the word "action."

The camera dolly glides along the rails that have been laid over the grass. It would seem that the director doesn't want to use the zoom lens. He's after a long, steady shot. An interminable shot.

"Don't stop," he murmurs in the cameraman's ear.

What can they have given the lamb to drink for it to stand so still? Probably a sedative, because now its knees bend and it slowly slumps, knocking over the glasses, which clink together, creating a crystalline music . . .

"That's good!"

"Perfect!"

"Unbelievable!"

The whole film crew is carried away, they're in ecstasy. The director rubs his hands together. And we actors applaud.

"A once-in-a-lifetime shot!" exclaims the director of photography.

"A real miracle!"

Another round of applause.

Everybody sits down at the table. Jean fetches some loaves and cans of sardines. We're hungry.

"Bring a lemon!"

François picks up the lamb. It's sleeping the sleep of the righteous. It's hot out here. They ought to turn off those arc lamps. What a waste of electricity! But the director is in a rush. So is the director of photography. He does a circuit of the table, holding his light meter.

"Sit a little closer together."

He is gesticulating, sweating. He is wearing a large red neckerchief.

"Lay the lamb on the table!" orders the director.

François carries out the order. Through clumsiness, he knocks over a bottle and the wine stains the lamb's fleece red. In a panic, the peasant looks right and left. Marc

sniggers. But the director's voice, amplified by the megaphone, reassures everybody:

"Never mind. Refill your glasses. Give me a little more
liveliness, for God's sake!"

Mathieu has to sing, accompanied by the accordionist:
a languorous tango. He crooks one arm and curls the
other, as if cradling a baby. Hamming it up . . .

"Action!"

Marc invites me to dance. He's stuck a peony in the but-
tonhole of his shirt. François is dancing with the makeup
artist. A dozen or so feet away, a circle of onlookers forms.
Among them is the stationmaster, who watches with great
interest. But the director isn't satisfied. He bellows into his
megaphone, so loudly that you can't understand a word.
And what with his accent! But the upshot is that we have
to do it again.

Mathieu sings and dances at the same time. He has
taken the makeup artist away from François and is dancing
with her, holding her tightly around the waist.

"You're hurting me," she whispers.

He thrusts his knee between her legs, resting his chin
on her shoulder, she groans, but does her best: she throws
her head so far back that her long hair brushes the grass.

"That's good!"

At a signal from the director, the stationmaster sits
down at the table, next to Jean. He refuses to eat any sardines. Jean pours him a drink. The stationmaster is feeling
unwell.

Jean raises his glass to drink.

"What's up, boss?"

"It's up . . . and it's down."

They drink. The music drowns out their words. The stationmaster stares at the lamb, which is still asleep.

As I dance, I take off my blouse and throw it on the grass. Marc is delighted.

Jean vanishes inside the bistro and returns with another table. This time, he is assisted by the two peasants, who carry the chairs. We're growing in number.

The accordionist changes the tune. He's now playing a folk melody unfamiliar to Mathieu, who is happy to take a break, however. He sits down at the table and Jean pours him some wine.

"What's up, boss?"

We clink glasses, drink, make merry.

I carry on dancing, with Marc and with others. The accordionist is now playing a lively gigue. How we stamp and whirl! Marc has unbuttoned his shirt, which now flaps around his chest. I've put the peony in my hair.

Jean brings more bottles. There are more than a dozen bottles lined up on the grass, with more on the table. They are tapping to the rhythm of the music with their knives and forks.

The stationmaster is cradling the lamb in his arms to protect it from the frenzied revelers. Splashed with wine, the lamb sleeps, oblivious. The director makes no objection. He is busy behind the camera, holding a bottle. Maybe he didn't even notice, the same as he doesn't notice that the stationmaster, still holding the lamb, is quietly slipping away. After walking for a few paces, he turns his head.

The camera is pointed at the woman, who, without a blouse, without a bra, is performing her idea of a belly dance. The others clap their hands in time to the music.

They egg her on, yelling and moaning. Somebody throws up.

The camera slowly moves closer, circles Marie as she dances in a passion.

IN THE BISTRO, Jean is busy behind the bar. The accordionist is the first to come in. The sound of the door closing comes immediately after the clapper board.

"The door, you chucklehead! Film the door not the bar," yells the director.

The cameraman is mortified. He apologizes.

"I've only just woken up . . ."

Hardly surprising, after yesterday's bender. They sank dozens of bottles. There behind the bistro, on the grass, where they had the picnic after filming, until late into the evening. "We'll throw a party in honor of the lamb," the director had said, and everybody agreed. As for me, I don't see what's so clever about filming a poor lamb plonked on a table piled with bottles and glasses. They had to tie it down so that it wouldn't move. But anyway, I didn't say anything. I cradled the lamb in my arms to protect it. The others drank, danced. Marie went wild: she took off her blouse and bra, her skirt was down below her belly button, she was twisting, turning, swaying her hips with oriental abandon. I couldn't take any more. I got out of there. Taking the lamb with me. I didn't feel well and, besides, I didn't like the heavy red wine they were drinking. Although the director loves it.

He shouts action through his megaphone, the clapper

board snaps, the door opens, and the accordionist bursts in.

"Hello, how's it going?"

"It's going all right," replies Jean. "Are you having anything?"

"Don't know, it's so hot . . ."

"If you're hot, go outside. Everybody else is outside."

The accordionist scratches the back of his neck. He picks up his accordion, which is resting at the foot of the bar, and says it's not a bad idea, but the cameraman misses this piece of action, which doesn't escape the vigilant eye of the director. They do another take.

I could have gone back up to my room, to bone up on the script some more, but I know it well enough by now; I've got it off by heart. I don't have to lug it around with me, like I did before. At any rate, I have enough time for a coffee. To tell the truth, I had a liver attack last night.

"You didn't!"

"Yes, I did."

"You drink too much," says Jean, commiserating with me.

I shrug. He adds:

"You need to lay off for a while . . ."

"Good idea," says the accordionist and goes outside.

"All right, let's do it again."

The accordionist comes back in through the front door.

Finally, it's my turn. According to the script, I should first have crossed the square and then stopped next to the monument to get out my handkerchief, take off my cap, mop my brow. But since there's no monument . . . I might well allude to the fact, but the director won't listen.

"Now for the next scene!"

He's in a rush, the bugger . . .

All right, I'm going out.

The next instant, the stationmaster comes in. He seems preoccupied.

"How's it going, boss?"

"All right . . ."

I go over to the bar.

"Give me something to drink, please."

"What would you like?"

"Fix me some lemonade or something . . ."

Jean looks at me in amazement. I at least owe him some kind of explanation. I say:

"I had a liver attack, last night . . ."

"You didn't!"

"Yes, I did . . ."

"No, you didn't!" shouts the director. "Cut!"

He comes up to me, fuming.

"Are you out of your mind?"

"Why? It's true . . ."

"What is truth? There's only one truth and it's me who decides what it is . . . Where's the script?"

Someone hands him the burgundy binder. He opens it, looks for the scene, doesn't find it, and looks at me, slightly disconcerted. As for me, I smile calmly.

"What is truth . . ." he repeats in a voice suddenly grown weary. "The script . . ."

He continues to look for the scene. I smile, because I know why he can't find it. But I don't say anything.

"Some pages are missing," he mutters. "Get me another script!"

He is given another copy. He searches, finds the scene

we shot yesterday, but not the one we're doing today. For the simple reason that in the script it comes before the one we did yesterday. He is too agitated to think straight. Jeanne-Marie and Marie-Jeanne attempt to explain it to him. The continuity girl tells him she thought the switching of the two scenes was deliberate. She takes the script, shows him the scene, yes, he was right, nothing about a liver attack. But there ensues quite a theoretical discussion, something I can't stand . . . The continuity girl complains about the lack of any continuity editing. Continuity editing? Yes. It's not enough to have just dialogue, she says. You can't embark on a feature-length film with just a three-page synopsis. Or even just . . .

"You're talking rubbish," says the director, in his own defense. "What do you mean a three-page synopsis? What about the script? There's a script . . ."

"Yes, of course, but what's happened is . . ."

"Don't exaggerate!"

"To have interesting subject matter, good continuity . . ." says the director of photography, sticking his oar in.

"On my head be it!" declares the director, with a kind of furious pride. He rubs his left earlobe, tugs it, twists it.

"For good continuity, what's needed above all else . . ."

"Why are you sticking your oar in?"

"All I wanted to say is that what's needed . . ."

"I didn't ask for your opinion. I'm sick of you, the whole lot of you! Well then! Do we have a script? Yes, we do! True, there's no need for one, but I was thinking of the actors. For them, a script is reassuring . . ."

"Not necessarily," I say, but he continues his muddled speech, now wielding his megaphone.

"For me, the ideal would be to draft the script only

after the film is finished. But for the actors . . . And the continuity . . . Why chop up the scenes into takes using a pencil? Is it to allow the director to express his personality? And to impose it on others in a pedantic, even peremptory way? But I, monsieur, I express myself directly, I hate pencils, biros, fountain pens and every pathetic instrument employed to set down in black and white what in reality appears in color . . ."

And so on, in the same vein, for a number of minutes in a row. We're all left open-mouthed, speechless, nobody dares interrupt him. He's the slave driver aboard this galley . . .

"So, are we doing another take?" asks the cameraman.

"Yes, we are."

He has regained his composure. His diatribe has done him good. He's even thinking about keeping my improvised line.

"A liver attack, that works," he says, and this time the continuity girl dares not gainsay him.

Jean fixes the lemonade. The stationmaster takes off his cap and unbuttons his uniform.

"Problems?" asks the bistro owner.

"No, nothing serious . . ."

"Tell me, is it true what Thomas says?"

The stationmaster does not answer straightaway. Jean hands him his lemonade. The stationmaster drinks. He's really thirsty. He wipes his mouth with the back of his sleeve. Jean goes back on the attack:

"Is it true?"

"What does he say?"

Jean seems a little embarrassed. He hesitates. It's obvious that the stationmaster doesn't feel like talking. The director doesn't interrupt us anymore.

"You know what a blabbermouth Thomas is . . . He's probably been telling fibs. But he's not a bad lad, Jean says. Not at all. Is he?"

"Thomas bad? Why?"

"I mean, he is when he lets his mouth run away with him . . ."

I drink, say nothing. We can hear the accordion and Mathieu singing.

"They're having fun!"

"Yes, real fun."

"But where has he gone?"

"Who?"

"Thomas. He's gone away, hasn't he?"

"Ah, yes. He left on the local train . . ."

"So what he said is true!"

"Said about what?"

"About the local train. He said that it won't be stopping at our station anymore."

I don't say anything else. Jean falls silent for a few moments, but then continues, unabated:

"They're mad, they are! Besides, how will people get to the sanatorium?"

I still say nothing. I toy with my empty glass. The music can be heard more loudly: the accordion and Mathieu's voice. A tango.

"They're having fun. Dancing."

"Yes, they're dancing."

I need to take a piss. After yet another pause, stipulated in the script, which the bistro owner seems to know by heart, he says:

"Is it true that they're planning to build an asphalt road through the forest?"

"That's what they say . . . But I don't really believe it. Although anything is possible . . ."

"But what then?"

"When?"

I can't hold out any longer! I break off the conversation and head for the back of the bar. I open the door to the WC.

"Cut!"

By now I've unbuttoned my fly. I hear the director's megaphone:

"Get a move on, you're not the only one who needs to go!"

I gaze at the stream of my urine, whose color alarms me.

THE STATIONMASTER IS in bed, wide awake. His eyes wander all over the room. He's waiting for something. And here it is: the alarm clock rings.

"Are these shots from the first scene?" asks Marie-Jeanne.

"More or less."

He's taciturn this evening, thinks the film editor. He prefers to give his speeches in the morning. Or the afternoon.

The stationmaster descends the stairs.

"How's it going, Jean?"

"It's going all right, boss. Slept well?"

"Yes, very well."

"Ready for your coffee?"

"Yes, thanks."

He sits down at a table.

In the next shot, the stationmaster, flag in hand, strolls along the platform. He stops for a few seconds to look in the direction of the forest. The noise of the forest will shortly be drowned out by the sound of a locomotive.

"We'll have to add the sound of beating wings," says the director. "Where did you put that lighter?"

Marie-Jeanne searches for the lighter, which, naturally, is right there on the editing table, within the director's reach.

"It's right there under your nose," she says.

The train enters the station. At the same time, Marc appears, running up, all out of breath.

"On the subject of beating wings," ventures the editor. "The eagle's cage still hasn't arrived."

The director calmly smokes his cigarette. From the train alight two peasants and, a few moments later, the telegraph operator.

"We have the parrot," says the director, turning his head toward Marie-Jeanne. But she maintains her composure; she takes off her glasses to wipe them.

The stationmaster waves his flag. In this way he signals his presence to Thomas, who is talking to Marc. The telegraph operator is holding a large parcel.

A young woman in blue jeans walks past, holding a rucksack. Nobody pays any attention to her. Except the director, who, with astonishing celerity, pauses on the image.

"She's not bad, is she?"

The editor is less enthusiastic. She finds the makeup artist too young for the part, but she nods her head nonetheless.

"She looks just like her, doesn't she?" persists the director.

"Maybe from a distance."

Marc would like to know what is in the parcel. But coming up to them, the stationmaster thrusts him aside and grabs Thomas by the arm.

"Have a good journey?"

"Yes, very good."

Mathieu walks up to them, with the two peasants. One of them, François to be precise, is holding a lamb in

his arms. The lamb is covered in red stains. On noticing
this, Thomas points his finger and the others burst out
laughing.

"Is that blood or paint?"

"You've guessed wrong . . ."

The stationmaster attempts to put a stop to it all, saying:
"Nonsense!"

"Let him try to guess . . ."

Thomas hands the parcel to the stationmaster, enabling
himself to bend over and sniff the lamb's fleece. He bursts
out laughing.

"The truth is always funny," remarks Mathieu.

"We had a great time," says Marc.

"A real ball!"

The telegraph operator is obviously sorry not to have
been there. The group start walking, heading away from
the station. Carrying the parcel, the stationmaster brings
up the rear. Only the camera and the young woman
remain behind. Both of them invisible.

The group crosses the small square and arrives in front
of the bistro. We see the signboard:

THE IMPERIAL EAGLE

"We'll insert some shots from scene nineteen here," says
the director. "From the bistro, when they were playing dice,
drinking, talking, joking. When Mathieu was singing."

"Again?"

Marie-Jeanne hesitates, but then she takes the bull by
the horns and voices her reservations:

"Maybe there's too much repetition . . ."

"Too much repetition?"

"Yes."

"There's too little!"

And the director pauses the projector and lights another cigarette. He repeats:

"Too little, you mean . . ."

"Here we go," thinks the editor, "he's about to get talkative. He's probably going to launch into one of his speeches. He'll start talking about Rivette or Robbe-Grillet again." But the director carries on smoking, pensively. "Maybe he'll start talking about how repetition is the mother of all cinema. Or about the text. Or about both." But he doesn't say any of all that, he smokes and smiles: "If repetition is the mother, then who's the father?" Marie-Jeanne pricks up her ears, takes out a cigarette, and says, "thanks," since the director has been prompt with his lighter. "Don't mention it," he replies. Silence ensues.

Abruptly, he presses play on the projector.

A woman, viewed from behind, descends a flight of steps leading to the terrace of a sanatorium. The patients, mainly women, are lying on chaises longues. They speak in German, but the sound is very faint. The music coming from the bistro down below is more clearly audible.

A stretcher is wheeled in on a hospital trolley.

"Where did you come up with all these shots?" asks Marie-Jeanne.

The director smiles but does not bother to reply.

The image shrinks until it can be seen to be playing on a television screen. Marie-Jeanne nods. So, it's in Marc's room. Marc is looking out of the window.

"Make a note: at this point you insert the men coming through the forest with the stretcher."

"Got it."

"And a few shots from scene twenty-two."

"Got it, boss."

"And from the terrace of the sanatorium . . . Although we haven't shot that yet."

"Yes you have," says the editor. And then, with a trace of irony: "Or don't you want any repetition?"

The director fails to detect the irony. Or maybe he does detect it, but doesn't give a shit. He returns to the image, saying: "On the terrace of a sanatorium, lying on a chaise longue, a woman who looks a little like Marie . . . But her face will be partly hidden by the book she is reading."

"What book?"

"It doesn't matter! *Waiting*, for example, or, if you like, *Exercises*."

"Why not *Exercises in Waiting*?" laughs the editor and pushes a button. The reel isn't finished.

"You have a point."

Marie goes up to the switchman, who's watching television, sitting on his bed.

A war film: soldiers with rifles and submachine guns, in a forest. A man runs along a path. A soaring eagle.

"I don't understand. When did you have the time to insert all this?"

The director remains silent. He lays his hand on the editor's arm. As if to reassure her.

"Have you been working through the night?"

He makes no reply.

Marie sits down next to Marc and ruffles his mop of hair. He puts his arm around her waist and attempts to push her backward onto the bed. Amused, she makes a show of resistance.

On the television screen: a woman waiting on a

stretcher, her eyes closed. Behind her, four soldiers with rifles slung over their shoulders.

Marc perseveres, trying to unbutton Marie's blouse. She now takes him seriously, fights tenaciously, and finally gains the upper hand: she repels her aggressor and stands up.

"Aren't you ashamed of yourself?"

The director looks at Marie-Jeanne, who patiently endures his gaze, waiting for him to look back at the screen so that she can look at him.

On the screen, a man who looks like the stationmaster is walking through the forest. We don't have enough time to be sure it is him, because he comes to a stop by a large tree and turns his back to us.

I'm stretched out on my bed, reading. It was Marie-Christine who gave me the book, saying that I had to read it, no doubt about it: it was better written and more specific than the screenplay. And since I know the screenplay almost by heart, I had nothing to lose: I told her to give me the book and I'd try to read it. In fact, this novella of his isn't at all bad. Despite its rather convoluted narrative style and over-heavy symbolism. It's the symbolism that annoys me the most.

It wasn't easy to carry the birdcage along the narrow corridor of the sleeping car, even though the train carriage was empty, everybody had alighted and now they were walking around on the platform or behind the station—the more adventurous ones had set off down the path that led through the forest, carrying their skis—or else they had sat down to eat in the waiting room or in Luca's room, since there were no seats in the restaurant car. The birdcage banged against the walls of the corridor, and taking fright, the bird was trying to spread its wings, jabbing its beak against the bars or through them, at the man's thigh, which luckily was encased in the thick blue cloth of his railway uniform. The woman brought up the rear and whenever the man

turned his head, an enigmatic smile appeared on her
face, the same smile as before, in the compartment,
when he had grown all flustered and tried to embrace
her, before realizing how ridiculous he was; her smile
was mechanical, as if at the push of a button a little
pink bulb lit up behind her forehead, illumining her
face and her blue eyes.

The alarm clock interrupts my reading. I get out of bed.
I do a few exercises in front of the mirror above the washbasin. I brush my teeth: my molar is still aching. In my
undervest, I carefully shave. I put on my uniform, my cap,
knot my blue necktie, take the flag, and leave the room.

In the corridor, Marie has just left her room, slamming
the door behind her. She runs to another room, tries to
enter, but the door must be locked. Marc also appears in
the corridor; he is in a state of heightened excitement. He
rushes after Marie, who is by now descending the stairs.

"Marc!"

He doesn't hear. He refuses to hear. He too vanishes
down the stairs.

Downstairs in the bistro, Mathieu is singing. Everybody
else sings along. Even the director joins in. Or else he
pretends to, because he opens and closes his mouth more
than the others. As soon as they see me, they give friendly,
mocking waves. I know, I know, I'm late. I raise my arms
and then let them drop: nothing I can do about it.

"Because of the alarm clock . . ."

My excuse is met with hilarity. But even so, it's true: I
set the alarm clock an hour late, because it had stopped.
That was my fault, obviously: I always forget to wind it
up. It's too complicated to explain all this amid the general

commotion. The director intervenes to put a stop to it.

"Back to work, right now!"

The same as every day, in the morning we prepare for the afternoon's filming. The director loves rehearsals. Today, it looks like he's catching up on a few small scenes: one in the bistro, one in Marc's room. I don't appear in any of them. They can very well film without me. Go on then! In any event, the director isn't complaining. But it amuses him to let the others heckle me. He rubs his hands together and shouts yet again:

"Everybody back to work!"

I feel like talking about his novella, like saying a couple of words to him about it, even if I haven't finished it yet. But it probably isn't the right moment. I find out that they've already filmed the scene in Marc's room. I didn't hear a thing. Although I wasn't asleep, I was reading. And here I am obliged to explain it all, that is, the alarm clock that was stopped and the rest . . .

"And what was it you were reading so passionately?" asks Mathieu. But the director comes past with his light meter and moves us apart, shouting: "Make way! Make way!" And he winks at me. He's in a good mood this morning.

The continuity girl pushes me aside, brusquely, humorlessly: she's completely devoid of humor! She pushes me into a corner to tell me that for once, I've tied my bootlaces, although this isn't marked in the script.

"But aren't we having lunch first?"

"I'm just doing my job," she declares and then turns her back on me.

I ought to have a cup of coffee and get back to my reading. My rôle this afternoon is minimal. As usual, I will be playing dice and glancing at the bar from time to time. I go looking for the director to tell him what I intend to do. But he is deep in conversation with Marie If You Please, who, as jittery as a flea, is listening to his instructions and nodding her head. From time to time, she gives a mechanical smile, as if at the push of a button a little pink bulb lights up behind her forehead, illumining her face and her blue eyes. I'm proud of my memory. He too would be proud to know that I have already learned by heart a number of passages from his text. But he doesn't look at me. He's only interested in the young woman, who moves her lips, trying to get a few words in edgeways, but the director's outpouring doesn't abate. Still talking, he bends his head and grasps her hand. It's true that she resembles Marie-Christine, and I can't help but think that if things keep heading in this direction, the actress will end up annoyed, even offended. There'll be ructions!

I order some coffee and François suggests a game of dice. He's obviously joking.

"Just for practice," he jests.

No, really, I'd rather go back up to my room. The cameraman is taking readings with his light meter. The continuity girl is marking crosses and circles on the floor with chalk. Mathieu and Jean are talking. Marie and Marc are not here. I decide to go back up to my room and continue reading.

Before she died, Maria said she didn't wish to be cremated at the sanatorium or buried in the nearby village; he had to carry her by stretcher to the next station down the line, on the other side of the forest, and transport her from there by train. But that only happened after the autopsy, which he couldn't dispense with, as the people at the hospital were adamant: it was in the interests of science, they said, and in any case, you have nothing to lose. In the end, he agreed to it, he sat down on a bench in the forest glade in front of the hospital and waited while science took a tiny step forward. An hour later, a nurse came up to him, red in the face, panting, and informed him that Marie's body had vanished from the autopsy room.

Somebody knocks loudly on my door. There's no doubt about it, director and writer don't make a good pair. The door opens and Marc sticks his beard inside to inform me that the director is looking for me everywhere.

"I ran all the way to the station," he says, entering the room, astonished to see me in bed. "What's with you? Are you ill?"

I show him the book and he guffaws, saying, "What on earth is that?" I get up and hold out the book, but he doesn't want to touch it.

"Don't be afraid, it won't bite . . ."

"Come on, we're wasting time!"

During lunch, the director solemnly announces that the filming has reached a crucial moment.

"Have we run out of money?" asks Thomas.

"No, at least I hope not. It's nothing to do with money."

And he points at Marie If You Please, the makeup artist, who blushes till her face turns scarlet.

The other Marie looks at me, livid.

"Don't take it to heart," I mutter.

"Does he want to screw her or what?" growls the actress and glares at me as if it were my fault.

"It's already happened," whispers Jeanne-Marie.

The director continues his tirade, with astonishing insouciance:

"Marie has been kind enough to agree to fight on two fronts: both in front of and behind the camera . . ."

His lyrical effusiveness ought to merit a round of applause. But unfortunately, he has not finished his speech. He lays it on even thicker, carried away by his enthusiasm. The way he talks, it's as if he placed the two Maries on an equal footing, and even demands the willing co-operation of the others and of Marie-Christine in particular, in view of Marie If You Please's inexperience in her new job; the worst has come to pass, and nobody is surprised when the actress makes a stormy exit. With one sweep of her script she sends flying her plate of fried potatoes, her glass of red wine, her knife, her fork, all of which land at the feet of the director, who sits rigid on his chair.

Despite this incident, filming carries on as planned. Tantrums must not hinder the forward march of a crew that has now almost reached the half-way point of the journey. Even though it looks like the clapper board man is the main character and Mathieu keeps losing his voice after so many takes. As for me, I'm starting to hate playing dice, as well as François's mouth.

"Are we playing?"

"Well . . ."

Marie vanishes out of the back door. Marc exclaims:

"Damn it!"

And he vanishes after her.

Nobody pays any attention to such mood swings. Everybody sings along with Mathieu.

"Are we playing?"

"Well . . ."

"Let's play!"

Mathieu can't take any more. The accordionist carries on alone, singing in a loud, shrill voice.

In the meantime, seemingly unnoticed (*dixit* the script), a woman enters the bistro a number of times: blonde, hair tied in a small bun, wearing quite faded blue jeans and an extravagant blouse. She holds a suitcase, larger and heavier each time she enters, which she places on the floor by the bar, with a sigh of relief. But her rucksack remains slung over her shoulder.

"Cut!"

"That's no good," says the continuity girl. "No good at all!"

The makeup girl is on the verge of tears. The director comforts her, strokes her cheek, her hair, her arms, her shoulders, her breasts, her hips . . . But in vain! She keeps making goofs, especially when it comes to saying her two or three lines as she stands at the bar.

"What will you be having?"

"Some milk . . . if you please."

"A grenadine!"

We keep going. What else can we do? Marie-Christine has shut herself up in her room. Marc plays the errand boy, going up and down the stairs, without success. She won't come out. The director himself has tried to cajole her: she still has her double rôle and, in any case, the voice has to be the same . . . they're only changing the . . . the figure. In vain. He can hardly tell her: the other woman is younger! So, we have to go on. It's getting late already. I wearily throw the dice.

"Look at that, a double six . . . What luck."

François lacks all enthusiasm too.

The newcomer, dare I say it, doesn't drink milk. That's calvados in her glass. Marc enters by the back door. He notices the young woman and comes to a stop. She senses his gaze and slowly turns her head away, looking to her left.

"Look at Marc, for God's sake! Over there, on the right . . ."

I cast the dice yet again. But before I do, I turn my head to glance for an instant at the young woman. No longer than an instant. Long enough for a flicker of interest to register in my eyes. The camera moves in, I'm in close-up, I know, but I'm falling asleep.

"Wake up!" bawls the director.

I ask for some water, to sprinkle my face. And a calvados!

"Look at that, a double six, what luck . . ."

The makeup girl is drinking at the bar. She senses the gaze of the switchman, who enters by the back door. She slowly turns her head away, to her left, and looks the cameraman straight in the eye. The director claps his hand to his brow, helplessly.

"Serves him right," whispers François, who has also ordered himself a calvados.

The accordionist alone is tireless. Jean refills the glasses. Mathieu starts singing again, with what little voice he has left. In the end, it's the camera that looks Marc straight in the eye. That's the solution!

"What about the transition?" mutters Jeanne-Marie.

It'll work! Marc climbs the stairs. From the top, he looks at the newcomer once more. And then at her rucksack, whose strange shape might inspire misgivings.

"What's inside it?" François asks me.

"A cage . . ."

"A cage for what?"

"A cage for . . . for a parrot."

But the director won't allow such kidding around. He says, "Cut!" then, "Action!" once more, then, "Cut!" once more, then, "Action!" once more . . .

Marc melts into the gloom of the staircase.

I WAKE UP early. Stretch, yawn. Tense my arms, my legs. Spread them, flex my knees. Suddenly, I remember that I have to be sad, downcast, because of that bastard director who thinks he can thumb his nose at contracts and basic decency. Who, in the middle of filming, doesn't hesitate to humiliate me, the star of the film. And all for what? For the sake of whom? For a wretched floozy! If he had at least warned me, if he had taken some kind of precautions, even if only rhetorical, if he had worn kid gloves . . . The cad! If he had explained it to me, given me his reasons, or even just said, Here's the thing, I'm having it off with this girl and I think there's a resemblance between the two of you . . . But he's a moron, if there's a resemblance between us, then . . . Idiot!

I'd do better to go back to sleep. To treat him with calm contempt. There's no point making a scene, he's not worth it, and he's certainly not worth swearing at. He's not worth a single word. I'll let them trot up and down the corridor, him and his whole pathetic film crew, I'll keep my door locked, and then I'll pack my bags and leave. Without a single word!

Yesterday, when he came to cajole me, to assure me that it only had to do with a partial dubbing, what did he mean by a change of figure?

Somebody tries the door handle, knocks.

"Open up, for God's sake! We need to talk."

It's him. Get lost!

"Open up, Marie, I'll explain everything. There's been a misunderstanding."

I don't budge. He knocks once, twice, then goes away. Go to the devil! I get out of bed and stand in front of the washbasin to look at myself in the mirror. I'm looking good: I had a good night's sleep. I go over to the window. In the square in front of the hotel, a group consisting of Marc, François and Thomas is looking up at my window. Marc stretches out his arm, I step back, close the shutters.

Another knock on the door. I smile and open the cupboard. Inside I see a copy of the script, I pick it up and hear the weary, rather nasal voice of J. C.

"Open up, Marie. It's me."

In reply I hurl the script at the door. I start getting dressed, without haste, I have all the time in the world.

"You can't do this to us. Without you the film will be ruined!" moans poor J. C.

I know that very well. But they should have thought of that before. And that wop in particular should have thought of it!

But how can I say such things. I feel bad about it: me, a woman of the left, letting myself get so carried away by anger . . . Luckily for him, because having erupted from my subconscious, the word "wop" triggers in my mind a reaction that ends up going in his favor. An inner voice comes to his defense: "It's his first film, quite unusual for an old duffer like him, it's his final book . . ."

"Open up, I beg you!"

He himself said it: "If I hadn't had the money, I would have written a novel." Is that so? In what language, pray tell? Yet another translation? Aimed at whom? At which audience? And who would have published this novel of yours? P.O.L.? Literature is finished, darling, nobody reads novels anymore, and if they do, then it's only beach novels. Or *romans de gare*, railway novels, to read on the train . . . People have other worries. They don't have the time. When they get home from work (or after a long day on the dole), they turn on the TV. That's more than enough for them!

"Marie, I beg your forgiveness . . ."

His voice is humble and despairing now. He must have realized what a stupid thing he's done. And now he's ruing the day. I feel myself starting to cave.

"Wait a moment! I'm getting dressed."

Sounds of rejoicing on the other side of the door. I can picture them hugging each other like soccer players after scoring a goal. How about I throw a little cold water on them?

"I'm getting dressed, but after that we'll have a serious talk."

"Whatever you want. You'll see, it was just a misunderstanding."

"What misunderstanding? Do you take me for a fool?"

Losing my temper again, I open the door. I see them laughing. I'm in my knickers. I close the door. I put on a flowery skirt and a very large man's shirt. No bra. I pick up the script and open the door again. The director steps up to me, holding out his hand.

"Shall we make our peace?"

"All right. But before that, you'll explain to me what's

been going on in that head of yours. And don't try to fob
me off again, telling me it was a misunderstanding."

"I promise. How about we go downstairs for a coffee?"

"Fine. But mind you! I'll accept your excuses only on
the condition that you give me a plausible answer. We're
not little kids . . ."

"You'll see."

And he rubs his teeth with his thumb.

Everybody is downstairs. Even the floozy. When they
see me coming down the stairs, they start cheering and
clapping. I lift my hand in a friendly wave. They're not the
ones to blame. I look at the makeup artist, who seems very
happy to see me. She's not to blame either. In her shoes,
bombarded by the flattery and reckless promises of that
man, even I would have . . . In her shoes, obviously! The
guilty party comes down the stairs behind me, as happy
as a lark. He waves his arms in the air like an orchestra
conductor. A bit of a loon . . .

But he's prepared his speech for the defense very well.
He explains to me that when it comes to a double rôle,
there are moments when not even the cleverest special
effects will suffice.

"Have you read the script carefully?"

What's this? Now he's trying to regain the upper hand?

"And what about the scene from yesterday?"

"You see, there's a resemblance between the two Maries,
but also a slight difference. When it comes to their figures,
for example . . ."

"Are you trying to suggest that I'm too fat?"

"No, not at all, you're perfect for your part. Which is
not that of a budding young girl, but rather a woman in
full bloom . . . Whereas she . . ."

"You mean to say that I'm no longer young?"

"No, all I'm saying is that she's ageless. Which is only natural . . ."

"Why?"

He hesitates for a few seconds. He looks to his left, to his right, and then leans toward me.

"She's dead . . ."

"Dead?"

He makes a sign for me not to speak so loudly. He whispers in my ear:

"She doesn't exist . . ."

I don't understand this at all well. The man is slightly deranged. Think of the poor audience. But ho hum. We make our peace, embrace. He whispers in my ear once more:

"Have no fear. I'll be there, at your side."

Then he stands up, as nimble as a rabbit, and in a self-confident voice, no longer looking at me, he cries:

"Everybody back to work!

We redo the scene from yesterday. The takes that Marie If You Please kept botching. Without Mathieu and the rest of the caboodle. They'll tie all the loose ends together in the editing room; it's hardly nuclear physics.

Jean gives me a business-like look.

"What will you be having?"

"Some milk . . . a grenadine."

We then get ready for the scene in the corridor. I alter my hair, to look like hers, put on a pair of faded jeans and a flowery blouse. She does my makeup. I evince no reaction when she smiles. Not yet, at least . . . I feel like asking her whether she has slept with . . . But I decide against it. At any rate, I have all the time in the world; she's not going anywhere. Not for a good while yet.

They have set up two cameras upstairs, in the corridor. One behind, for her, and the other at the other end, for me.

"Let's go!"

She takes me by the hand, leads me . . . Her hand is cold . . . They put the parrot's cage in her rucksack. She puts the straps over her shoulder. Walking alongside her, Jean carries the suitcase. Ready?

The corridor is narrow, the suitcase bumps against the wall. We have to do another take. They come to a halt in front of the door to my room and pretend to continue the conversation they began in the bistro.

"Cut!"

It's my turn. The rucksack is heavy. I can feel the frightened bird struggling inside the cage, jabbing its beak at the bars and at the fabric of the rucksack. We arrive in front of the door. I ask Jean:

"Is it far?"

"Not far . . . We have to go through the forest. Although not the whole forest."

I adopt a dreamy tone of voice.

"The forest . . ."

"It's in a glade . . ."

"It must be beautiful there . . ."

"Yes, it's not bad."

I picture the ultra-modern sanatorium. On the terrace, the patients are lying on differently colored chaises longues in the sun, attended by tall blond nurses in white smocks . . . On the lawn are parked countless Bentleys and Rolls-Royces . . .

In the meantime, Jean has opened the door, and we both enter the room.

"Here we are."

He has the voice and manner of the consummate hotelier. I put the rucksack on the floor.

"Stop! There's no camera in there."

"That's cinema for you. A hash . . ."

"Beef hash," adds Jean.

J. C. congratulates us. He's less placid than usual.

"You're very beautiful today . . ."

"I'm the other one."

"Sorry?"

They move the bed to set up a camera and lights in its place. We go out, to have a drink. I'm hungry.

"We're ready, let's go!"

"Clapper board!"

"Action!"

Jean opens the door and we enter the room.

"Here we are."

He has the manner of the consummate hotelier. I put the rucksack on the floor. I have to release the bird, which is to say, I have to take the cage out, in fact no, not yet. I sink into a chair.

"I'm so tired!"

"This is Marie's room. We'll bring up another bed."

"A mattress will do."

He takes a few steps across the room. Overdoes it. I'm really tired. Jean continues:

"There's a shower at the end of the corridor."

"Thank you very much."

"Don't mention it."

Jean looks at me quite insistently. I stare into space.

And it's still not the end. We're doing overtime. Even though it's late already, our dinner is just a sandwich and we shoot another scene. We'll have a big supper and a lie-in tomorrow morning. This scene has the same atmosphere as scene fifty-two, Jeanne-Marie informs us. Except it's more languid. All the better! The accordionist plays a slow number. It sounds like he's improvising. He's fed up too . . .

The stationmaster has just finished a game of dice. He's about to leave, like the other customers in the bistro.

Behind the bar, Marie is doing the dishes. She seems different, tenser than usual, sterner. Naturally, she is annoyed that Jean has given a room to the newcomer. He might have warned her, at least. Jean attempts to mollify her.

"You know full well that there aren't any vacant rooms."

"I didn't say anything."

"But you do understand, don't you? Do you understand the situation? And besides, she's nice. We ought to help her . . ."

Mathieu goes up to the bar and says to Jean:

"Say, is it true that she's ill?"

"I suppose so. Otherwise, why would she be going to the sanatorium?"

"Don't ask me . . . Maybe she's going to work there as a nurse, a stretcher bearer . . ."

That irks Marie.

"Stop it!"

But he doesn't look at her. He's still speaking to Jean.

"Did you ask her?"

"Ask her what?"

"Whether she's going to the sanatorium?"

"She was the one who said . . ."

"Maybe she's coming back from there."

Marie interrupts once more. She's annoyed. The accordionist stops playing. He's going home.

"Goodbye, everybody!"

"So long."

"Bye. See you tomorrow."

Marc lies in wait at the top of the stairs.

We still have to do a scene in which the stranger takes from her rucksack a cage with a bird inside. What kind of bird? Difficult to say. We can't see, because the young woman is standing between the bird and the camera.

His face in close-up once more. His focused gaze. Then the bed, the stationmaster's body lying on the bed as if on a stretcher. A book falls off the bed.

The wall.

The stationmaster is now looking in the mirror above the washbasin. This time he doesn't pull a face. This time he doesn't smile. He runs his hand over his cheeks. He needs to have a shave.

"That's good," says the director. "Cut it there!"

Marie-Jeanne works with rapid, business-like movements. She cuts, splices, makes a remark about the book on the floor by the bed.

"It's his bedside reading . . ."

The director makes no reply. The film editor smiles.

The stationmaster looks out of the window. The sky is overcast. Before long, it will start raining again.

The stationmaster takes an album out of the cupboard. More than likely, he is looking for a specific photograph, because he flips the pages quickly.

Here it is: on the terrace of a sanatorium, a woman lies on a chaise longue, reading. Her face is completely hidden by the book.

And then everybody goes into the corridor.

"Are we keeping this bit?"

"Why not?"

They already have quite a few versions of it, but the director turns a deaf ear. You'd think he needed every single take!

But anyway. The stationmaster walks down the corridor, holding the flag. He comes to a stop in front of a half-open door. Through the crack in the door, we glimpse a woman lying on the bed. But it is hard to make out her body in the gloom, because the shutters are closed. The stationmaster stands motionless for a few seconds, leaning toward the door. It's quite . . .

"Isn't this too much?"

"No, not at all. Don't forget the sound of rustling leaves . . ."

"As if lots of people . . ."

"Four people!"

". . . were walking through a forest."

"Right."

He stands up and, without a word, leaves the room. Marie-Jeanne smiles. He's got the squirts! Hardly any wonder given all the plonk he guzzles. Serves him right, she mutters to herself. But the director returns more quickly than she expected. He restarts the projector. The stationmaster comes downstairs for a coffee. Another one? Jean is in a bad mood. He doesn't feel like making small talk.

"How's it going, Jean?"

"It's going all right."

"Is it raining?"

"Looks like it."

He makes the stationmaster's coffee, tight-lipped.

"With a drop of milk, please."

The stationmaster drinks his coffee, steps over to the

door, and without opening it peers through the pane of glass. It is indeed raining.

"Hurry up!" shouts the director. "It might stop at any moment. And he rushes down the stairs."

"Are we keeping that bit?"

The director makes no reply. He's not in any mood to make small talk, either. And besides, he's not partial to that kind of humor. Marie-Jeanne detects his annoyance and works quickly, as if to redeem herself.

He reaches the platform, taking long strides. The camera is already there, in Thomas's office. It's still raining: a heavy drizzle. The stationmaster is armed with an umbrella and the flag, his constant companion. Jeanne-Marie waves frantically at the conductor of the train pulling into the station.

"What are you doing? Are you asleep?"

"*À la gare comme à la gare . . .*"

"Come on!"

Marie-Jeanne makes Jeanne-Marie vanish. And now the director himself is running desperately along the platform. One might take him for a passenger without any luggage, for somebody trying to catch the last train.

"You should keep that shot, as a signature, à la Hitchcock . . ."

The director refuses to be provoked. In any event, he isn't happy with all these takes filmed in the rain, either. Even if the director did have a kind of rail laid from the telegraph office to the railroad track, the cameraman dawdled and was late in emerging.

"Come out of there already!"

"I was waiting for the signal."

"Shut it!"

"Yes, well . . . anyway . . ."

You can't stand around gabbing in the rain for long. The train reverses back up the tracks and then enters the station yet again, to be greeted by the lone stationmaster, who raises his flag, but so nonchalantly that the director feels like shouting "cut!" But he refrains. He's sick of it all, too.

Nobody boards the train, which then departs. The mechanic makes a hand signal and mouths something: probably a swear word. The stationmaster lowers his flag and heads toward the telegraph office, or rather toward the camera, which backs away before him, like a lion before its trainer. Or quite the opposite, thinks the director: you can train a lion while backing away from it . . .

It won't stop raining. The sky is like a gray belly . . . No. *A huge, whitish-gray belly.*

"How's it going, Thomas?"

"Not bad. But not good either."

Marc runs past, behind the stationmaster, who turns his head. The switchman keeps on running.

"Marc!"

But he doesn't stop. He runs around the clump of peonies, behind the storeroom.

"The rascal! Did you see that?"

"Yes, I saw it."

The camera is now pointed at the forest. In fact, *the clouds had drifted apart and were no longer so dense. A pinkish light had lit up over a section of the forest.*

"That's enough for today."

"Is it true that we need to read your story?" asks the film editor, stopping the projector.

"What story?"

"Your novella, of course! The one in the book . . ."

He shrugs.

"Why should you read it?"

"The better to understand the film . . ."

He was soaked to the skin. At the hotel, he ordered boiled wine with sugar, vanilla, cinnamon, and pepper.

He felt like going to sleep.

BEHIND THE BAR, I wash the dishes.

Marc bursts in, all out of breath, soaking wet. He shakes himself, his mop of hair spraying drops of water. He stamps his feet on the floor.

He sits down at a table and asks for a drink.

"A big glass!"

Marie fetches it without a word. He attempts to stroke her thigh but fails, because she dodges and then takes refuge behind her zinc-topped rampart, where she carries on washing the dishes.

"Drop the glass!" shouts the director.

How impatient he is! I was just about to drop it, I hadn't forgotten.

"A big glass!" repeats Marc.

Marie brings him it, but doesn't let herself be caressed. She's in a bad mood. Or rather she's preoccupied. She's thinking about the other Marie. She drops a glass and it breaks.

"*Merde!*"

"Marie . . ."

Marc's voice is faint, timid. Marie makes no reply. She doesn't look at him. He stands up and goes to the back of the room.

It's still raining. Marc looks out at the rain, at the grass in the rain, at the hills looming in the distance. He goes over to the bar and attempts to rest his elbows on the counter, the better to look at Marie, but given how short he is, it makes him look ridiculous.

"Perfect!"

Whether satisfied or dissatisfied, the director is always shouting. He bursts our eardrums with that megaphone of his, which he employs even when we're filming indoors.

I deign to look at Marc's bearded face, at his dark eyes, which are now astonished, now worried, and finally I relent. I stroke his still-wet hair, the way you might stroke a dog or a lion, scratching its fur.

In the next take, the jukebox is playing a sad song. People are drinking, playing dice. Jean and Thomas are whispering at the bar.

"Any news?"

"No, nothing."

"But they can't cancel the train service without notice. Without warning."

"No, of course not."

The camera is now pointed at the stationmaster, who shakes the dice in his fist for a long time before vigorously casting them. Too vigorously: the tumbling dice roll off the table onto the floor. I expect he did it deliberately, to goad the director a little. But the director appears delighted.

"Carry on! Carry on!"

"Sorry, says the stationmaster. Shall I do it again?"

"That was good, that was good!" shouts the director through his megaphone.

Everybody is searching for the dice on the floor. The hand-held camera follows them. The stationmaster alone sits still. He listens to the sad music on the jukebox, smiling vaguely.

Later, we go upstairs to film. First in Marc's room: he sits watching television, holding a rifle.

"Did you make a note of that? Shots from scene forty-nine," yells the director to the continuity girl, who is standing right next to him. Jeanne-Marie jumps; she has an earache. The man is insane. She prods her temple with her index finger. Offering no apology, he says:

"I need to go to the bog. My guts are in turmoil."

And so we wait. What else can we do? I ask Jeanne-Marie what shots he was talking about, and the continuity girl smiles in some embarrassment before answering.

"Nothing much . . . He brought an entire reel with him, and he gleans scenes from it . . ."

"What scenes?"

"Just scenes . . . I don't even know myself. Marie-Jeanne is the one who knows."

I see Marie-Jeanne and ask the same question. She gives me a detailed answer, describing a scene in which some German soldiers enter a bistro, ask for drinks, and eye up the woman behind the bar.

"She looks like Marie If You Please."

"No kidding!"

"I swear!"

"Is that why he chose her?"

"No doubt about it."

"But what's the film? Do you know?"

No, Marie-Jeanne doesn't know anything more than that. The director comes back. He's in a hurry.

"Everybody back to work!"

By now, Marie If You Please is in her room, or rather

mine. I knock on the door and it's my voice that asks: "Who is it?" Hilarious. I reply, altering my voice slightly.

"It's me!"

All for nothing, because I expect they'll redub it afterward.

The camera captures Marie getting dressed. She puts on her skirt, looks in the mirror above the dresser. She has magnificent breasts.

"Come in then!"

I enter. I pause on the threshold, admiring her.

"What a lovely dress you have!"

My voice sounds a little forced, but I couldn't care less. Marie puts on her blouse and plants herself in front of me so that I can get a better look. I'm better dressed than I was in the first scenes, too. More carefully dressed, at any rate.

"Feeling better?"

"I slept very well."

I move closer to her. I'm supposed to look at her tenderly, stroke her cheeks. The director has been quite dreading this scene, but he needn't have, the moron. I don't have anything against Marie If You Please; I don't have anything against anybody. I look at Marie—the camera curves its way around toward us—I gaze at her tenderly, I stretch my hands toward her face. What if I slapped her? No, it's not serious, which is to say, not even perverse . . . If we were onstage, in a theater, it might be exciting. But during filming . . . A minor scandal, explanations, excuses, and then another take. And besides, I've got nothing against her. I find her pretty, too pretty, right now, under the lights. And it's true that she resembles me . . . I stroke her cheeks.

"You're so gentle, so kind . . ."

In reality, she merely opens her mouth and moves her lips. It's all I can do to stop myself laughing.

"You're beautiful."

"So are you!"

I take her by the shoulders and draw her to the window. I stroke her shoulders, her arms. She has very soft skin. I glimpse the cage in one corner.

"It's stopped raining."

"You can stay longer. You know . . . it's not the right time to go walking through the forest."

I can't remember which of us has to kiss the other. I waver for a short space. Finally, it's she who kisses me, on the neck. She nibbles my neck. I throw my arms around her and wait for the famous "cut!", but he must be savoring the spectacle, the jackass, because he remains silent, everybody remains silent. I no longer even hear the whirring of the camera, and all of a sudden, they burst into applause. I turn my head, bewildered.

"That was good!"

"Perfect."

"Marvelous!"

The stationmaster looks the most enthusiastic. He kisses me, whispers congratulations. He smells of calvados. I'm still holding Marie If You Please's hand, which is sweaty with delight. We go downstairs. We have a drink in the bistro. During which time the director pays another visit to the jakes. His cap askew, his face more and more scarlet, the stationmaster looks at the two of us in satisfaction. The director returns, buttoning up his fly.

"You were in top form!"

And we get back to work. We go back upstairs. This

time the camera stays outside the room, in the corridor. The two of us go back inside the room, strip naked, and each of us lies down on her own bed. The door is wide open and Marc devours us with his eyes. But the cameraman chases him away, the better to position his camera. It has to be filmed as if somebody were spying through the keyhole: the classic ploy!

"Lie down on the same bed," yells the director through his megaphone.

Marie comes and lies down on my bed. She is completely naked; her breasts jiggle.

"Hug each other!"

I feel Marie's mouth on mine. She's not acting. She suffocates me, thrusts one knee between my legs. Was that really necessary? She lies on top of me, completely covering me. Won't the audience see nothing but her ass?

No, because she releases my mouth, my face, in order to bite my neck. Ow, you're hurting me! She slides lower, battens on my breasts. Like a greedy infant.

"That's enough!"

Amplified as it is, the director's voice does not immediately dampen the desire of my partner, who is now licking my tummy with her thick, violaceous tongue, the sight of which excites me more than all the previous kisses. I feel all hot and now I'm encouraging her by circling her hips with my legs, I feel like shouting at them to get that camera out of here and shut the door behind them.

SITTING AT A table on his own, Mathieu watches me come downstairs. I feel as light as a feather . . . He must be thinking how cheerful the stationmaster looks. How exhilarated, even.

"How's it going, Jean? Hello, Mathieu!"

"It's raining," replies Mathieu, and the stationmaster smiles, goes up to the bar, and orders his coffee.

"With a drop of milk," he says.

Jean serves me, his movements mechanical.

"Is it true? Are they cancelling the local train?"

I look at him without my smile fading.

"No, that's not it. Quite simply, the local train won't be making any more stops at our station."

"But that's stupid!"

"Yes, it is . . ."

"What about the sanatorium?" asks Mathieu, who gets up from his table and joins us at the bar.

"I don't know anything about that . . ."

"But how will people get to the sanatorium?" insists Mathieu.

"It seems that the sanatorium will also . . ." murmurs Jean, his head slightly bowed, as if he were looking at Jeanne-Marie's knees.

"Will also what?"

"But I don't know . . . Maybe there won't be a sanato-rium anymore."

"No, that can't be!"

"Why can't it be?"

Having finished his coffee, the stationmaster no longer has the patience to engage in idle chatter.

"Listen, my friends, I have to go. I'm late."

And he shows them his flag.

With resolute steps, he goes out. The other two men are left open-mouthed. They look through the glass pane of the front door at the receding outline of the stationmaster and then turn back to look at the camera, which plainly annoys the director: he dislikes even the slightest com-plicity between actors and audience. And as if that weren't enough, he also has a bellyache. Through his megaphone he yells a fateful "cut!" I take advantage of this to come back inside and order a calvados. Jean serves me at a table.

"Action!" bawls the director and Jean runs back behind the bar. Without any transition, he attempts to recompose the facial expression he was wearing in the previous take: he cranes his neck and parts his lips. Mathieu does like-wise. They stare at each other, like actors in a silent film. They boggle their eyes at each other. I think they're ham-ming it up, but the director makes no comment. He tugs and twists his earlobe.

"Late? But . . ."

"That's right. He ought to be over there!"

I'm not entirely sure whether Mathieu is really com-plaining or whether he's pulling our leg.

"To do what?"

"To salute, that's what!" And he raises his arm, holding

an imaginary flag. But he clenches his fist, and the director is not at all satisfied. He explains how to make such
a gesture without laying yourself open to a different kind
of interpretation.

"What kind of interpretation?"

"A political one, for example."

Mathieu doesn't understand, or pretends not to. He
says he's holding a flag.

"You're not holding anything, you're just pretending,"
says the director, and I get the impression that he now
has less of an accent. Then, despite his griping bowels,
he launches into a diatribe against realistic acting. He
talks about the estrangement effect, and even though he's
not very keen on Brecht, he says he still prefers him to
Stravinsky.

"You want me to give an open-palmed salute?"

"No, that would be even worse. You haven't understood
a thing . . ."

"Show me then, show me how you want me to do it."

The director takes the actor's place, says the line, but
without clenching his fist: he merely flexes his knuckles,
as if the stem of the flag were about to slip from between
his fingertips. But what about the flag itself, the small red
rectangle of cloth?

"All right," says Mathieu. "Now I get it."

Marc slowly descends the stairs. He shuffles his feet more
heavily than usual. He takes a seat at a table, downcast.

"A big glass, please."

Jeans asks Mathieu, who is doing finger exercises:

"What's up with him?"

The singer's hand looks more like a claw. He raises his

eyebrows and carries on with his exercises. Marc hides his face in his hands.

"Everybody back to work!"

On the station platform, the stationmaster makes a dignified salute to the local train, which passes without stopping. He continues to hold the flag high until the train vanishes among the hills. He then walks toward the camera, toward the telegraph office, toward Thomas, who is standing in the doorway.

"Where's that rascal got to?"

Thomas has no idea. In any event, he can't understand why I'm smiling.

It's raining.

Marc enters the bistro, soaking wet. He climbs the stairs without looking at Jean and Mathieu, who are talking at the bar. He seems livelier than before. But in the corridor, he comes across the entire film crew, who are resolutely waiting for him, behind the camera. Holding her notebook, Jeanne-Marie signals for him to hurry up. He quickens his pace and comes to a halt in front of Marie's room. The door is ajar. He looks through the crack in the door, but can't see very much: the birdcage and a woman's leg, up to the knee. And then another leg, on the bed. It's as if these two woman's legs were glowing . . .

Retracting his head from the crack in the door, he looks all around him. Nobody there. He crouches down and carries on spying. Cautiously, he opens the door a little wider and it gives a slight creak. He now sees three legs on the same bed.

At the end of the corridor, the stationmaster makes his appearance. His gait is rather stiff. He walks up to Marc, who seems enthralled by what he sees, and taps him on the shoulder.

"What are you doing there?"

Marc turns his head and grimaces. He points at the door.

"It was open . . ."

"Aren't you ashamed? You son of a bitch! Scram!"

He shoves him. Marc loses his balance and falls sideways. He picks himself up straightaway, furious. But he doesn't dare fight back. What could he have done anyway? Beaten me up? He walks away, swearing to himself. He enters his room and the director seems delighted. He gestures for me to carry on.

"Son of a bitch!"

But Marc is no longer there.

The stationmaster shakes his head. He leans toward the door to listen. The only sound is vague whispers and the rustle of sheets.

He shrugs, closes the door, and enters his own room.

I look out of the window. It's raining. A peasant enters the bistro. He is cradling a lamb.

WHEN THE DIRECTOR lets slip his first fart, Marie-Jeanne naturally makes no comment. She wrinkles her nose, knits her brow, and presses a button: the makeup girl comes down the stairs, holding a bowl. At the bottom of the stairs, Marc begins to ascend, rather gingerly. Fearfully, even. They pass on the stairs. She smiles at him. But he lowers his head and continues to climb, hugging the wall. Having reached the top, he pauses to look back downstairs: Marie If You Please is standing at the bottom, dithering, with the bowl in her hand.

The director farts again. This time it really stinks. The film editor pinches her nose between thumb and forefinger. She is obliged to breathe through her mouth. She still makes no comment.

Marc walks down the corridor. In front of Marie's door, he hesitates for an instant, bends over as if to look through the keyhole. He presses the door handle and enters. The bed is unmade. Next to it is an open suitcase, full of clothes. More clothes hang over the backs of the chairs. He picks up a blouse and sniffs it. Then he sees the cage. He tosses the blouse on the bed and approaches the cage taking small steps. For a long while he stares at the gilded bars, at the parrot, or rather the blue, yellow, and red toucan. The bird appears to be rigid.

Marie-Jeanne notices that the director is clutching his belly. She would like to make some ironic remark about the tricolored eagle, tell him that everybody is outraged at the eagle's replacement.

"If you can't omit this scene, then at least don't show the bird. Wait just a little bit longer, the delivery will arrive in the end," says the film editor, just as Marc kicks the cage.

"I know what I'm doing," the director replies calmly, his left hand searching for his bottle of plonk.

You have to be out of your mind to make films, thinks Marie-Jeanne, taking off her glasses to wipe them. He could at least have dyed the feathers, she says to herself. Dyed them gray, to make it more realistic. And not to disturb the actors. After that, once the eagle arrives, the real bird . . .

But even so, little Marc is afraid. He kicks the cage and straightaway retreats. He does so as if there were a real eagle in the cage. It's good acting. He looks around him. He needs a stick, some kind of long object. He looks in the cupboard: a coat hanger! He picks it up, approaches the cage once more, hesitantly. He snickers and prepares to strike. But just at that moment, Marie enters the room.

"What do you think you're doing? Are you nuts?"

"I was going to . . ."

"Get out of here or I'll call the boss. Out! Beat it!"

Marc is taken aback. He nevertheless gives the bars of the cage a tap with the coat hanger. Marie intervenes, pins his arms, and thrusts him toward the door.

"Get the hell out! Beat it, you son of a bitch!"

"Marie . . ."

"Go on, beat it!"

"But . . ."

Marie finally manages to shove him out of the room.

The director lets slip another fart, louder and more malodorous than the previous ones. Marie-Jeanne can no longer remain silent.

"Go to the toilet!"

The director remains calm. He raises the bottle to his lips and drinks without looking away from the small screen: Marie holds a bowl of water and a plate of mince-meat. She slowly climbs the stairs.

It doesn't make any sense, thinks the film editor. A parrot doesn't eat meat . . .

Marie enters the room with the food. The other Marie is sitting on the bed.

"He must be hungry."

She puts the meat inside the cage.

"He's grown bigger . . ."

"The cage will soon be too small for him . . ."

Marie stands up and strokes Marie's hair.

Marie-Jeanne changes the reel.

"It doesn't make any sense . . ."

The director looks for his lighter.

"Where is my lighter?" he says, but Marie-Jeanne makes no reply.

Marc gazes at the green field behind the bistro. It has stopped raining, but the sky is still overcast. Marc is holding a rifle. He waves it, with a disappointed look on his face. He walks away, over the field.

The stationmaster is looking out of the window. Behind him, on the table, is a vase of peonies. Somebody knocks on the door.

"Come in."

Marie enters; with a rather strange smile on her face,

which is more heavily made up than usual, she looks younger.

"How's it going?"

The stationmaster seems slightly abashed. He gestures vaguely.

"It's going all right. How about you?"

She walks up to him, strokes his cheeks.

"Why are you always unshaven?"

The stationmaster says nothing. Marie smiles. She is hiding something in her left hand, which she presses to her chest.

"Here . . ."

She shows him a small framed photograph, the one we have already seen on the stationmaster's bedside table. She hands him the photograph.

"Here . . ."

"Thank you, Marie!"

The stationmaster is touched. He stands there awkwardly, not knowing where to put the photograph. He gazes at her for a long moment. Finally, he puts it on the bedside table.

"How about here?"

"Yes."

The two of them look out of the open window. A slight breeze ruffles their hair, Marie's long blond hair in particular.

"A nice scene," murmurs Marie-Jeanne and glances at the director, who, with his hands folded over his belly, seems to be asleep.

And then, on the station platform, the stationmaster, carefully dressed, freshly shaven, his boots laced up, walks with an air of dignity. He even struts a little. He is comical.

Behind him, Marc pulls faces. The stationmaster does not see him, and even if he did see him, he wouldn't care. He strolls with his hands behind his back, his eyes fixed on the forest, as usual.

François now arrives, cradling the lamb. To a perceptive eye, the wine stains are still visible on the lamb's fleece, even if the peasant has taken pains to wash it.

"Hello there!"

Marc makes no reply. He carries on looking at the stationmaster. He no longer pulls faces. He is sooner fascinated by the stationmaster's pomposity.

"Hold the lamb for a minute, will you? I'm off for a piss . . ."

François places the lamb in Marc's arms. Deep in dumbfounded admiration, Marc makes no protest. The peasant now looks at the stationmaster, but isn't so impressed. He shrugs and crosses the tracks. He enters the forest.

Why does he make the sign of the cross?

In the doorway of his office, Thomas has a slightly dreamy air about him. He goes up to the stationmaster, who has ceased his strolling in order to study Marc, still motionless, cradling the lamb. The lamb bleats and Marc gives a start. He takes a few steps in the direction of the tracks. He comes to a halt, turns around. Thomas and the stationmaster burst out laughing.

Thomas and the stationmaster are watching television. It looks like a war film, but they are chuckling. On the small screen, a soldier plays the accordion. Another soldier attempts to put a hawk inside a cage. Other soldiers drink beer, served by a young blond woman who looks like the makeup girl. Oh what a lovely war!

"Are you keeping all this?"

By way of reply, the director lets rip with a miasmal fart and Marie-Jeanne chokes with indignation. She can't take any more.

"You're going to shit yourself any second now," she snaps, getting up. She goes out, slams the door behind her, without hearing the calm reply of the director, who at long last agrees with her.

In Marie's room, the two women are seminaked. They are trying on dresses. I can see them through the crack in the door. They often leave it ajar. Perhaps the director insists on it. Marie puts on the other Marie's dress, rather an elegant number.

"Oh, how pretty it is!"

"Yes, it suits you. But try on the other one. It will suit you better."

Obediently, Marie gets completely undressed.

"Your breasts are beautiful!"

"A little on the large side, aren't they?"

"Not at all!"

Marie lets herself be caressed. She glances at the cage. The bird is hopping about behind the bars. It obviously doesn't have enough room.

"It's often like that: after breastfeeding, they sag a little . . ."

"But I like them."

She cups one of Marie's breasts in both hands, places her lips around the nipple.

"Greediguts!"

Marie gently pushes away the other Marie's head and kisses her forehead, her eyes.

"Now it's your turn!"

She looks inside the dresser and takes out a dress longer than the others, made of white satin. A wedding gown? She shows it off with rather naïve pride, but also with slight embarrassment.

"Look . . ."

How the stationmaster loves the rustle of gowns! That was what he was listening out for, on the other side of the door . . .

"See this? Moths . . ."

"I really like it. It reminds me of so many things."

"Ah, memories!"

"Would you like me to do your hair?"

"Yes, very much."

The makeup girl lets her do her hair. When she has finished, the two women look even more alike. They are almost identical. Granted, one is younger, but even so . . .

The stationmaster goes downstairs to the bistro. He adopts a pompous mien, and his gait, which is still quite stiff, might even appear ridiculous. In any event, he is in a good mood. He smiles at Marc, who has just entered, cradling the lamb.

Behind the bar, Marie looks very young.

The director rubs his hands together and busies himself around the camera. He is constantly redoing the shot and this annoys the cameraman, who thinks there is nothing wrong with the previous takes. He hates being bossed around and above all he hates the director's manner. But I know that the director, far from being a perfectionist, is quite simply taking advantage of the repeated takes in order to admire the actress, whose makeup he himself did just now. In the camera frame, she's all his. Here he is adjusting the lighting, putting the poor bewildered electricians through hell.

"More light," he murmurs, dispensing with the megaphone for once.

The lighting technician doesn't hear him clearly, or else the director himself doesn't say it clearly, and so he has no right to blow his top when one of the spotlights goes out.

"Where's my megaphone?" he yells and starts looking everywhere, like Richard III in search of a horse.

Everybody rushes to look for the megaphone. I take the opportunity to order a glass of calvados.

"Make it a large one . . ."

Jean chuckles, Mathieu shakes his head, Marc orders himself a drink too. He gives Marie an insolent look.

"Can't you put that lamb down for one second?" she says.

"What if it runs away?"

"You catch it by the tail," says Jean.

And Marie laughs.

In the next instant, Jeanne-Marie emerges from the toilet, triumphantly holding the megaphone.

"I've found it."

"Was that where it was?" marvels the director, busying himself around the camera once more.

"More light," he bellows and glares at the lighting technician with his blue eyes. "Fetch another arc light!"

"Another one?"

"Yes. Two!"

Finally, the signal is given, the clapper board does its little routine, the director utters the word "action!", the whole shebang, all so that the rejuvenated Marie can say the following:

"Stop being stupid, Marc."

Marc goes out of the back door, cradling the lamb. He tethers the lamb to the door handle, comes back inside, and goes upstairs.

"Stop being stupid, Marc."

The stationmaster climbs the stairs behind him, comes to a halt at the top, gets down on all fours, and cranes his neck the better to survey Marc, who, in front of Marie's door, has glued his eye to the keyhole. He cannot see the birdcage, which is covered with frocks. Beneath the frocks, the parrot is asleep. Marc presses the door handle, but the door is locked. He retraces his steps. The stationmaster goes downstairs in front of him, moving backward.

At the bar, Thomas is talking to Marie in a low voice. We hear only long whispers and, from time to time, Marie's titters of laughter. The director is a little jealous. Wielding his light meter he goes over to break up the tête-à-tête. What is it that he wants, in fact?

"Everybody back to work," he shouts and tells Thomas to talk more loudly.

"Will do, boss!" replies the telegraph operator.

Without interrupting the filming, the director goes to the toilet once again. He takes the megaphone with him, naturally.

"Louder!" he yells, seated on the toilet bowl.

The stationmaster plays dice with François, but he's sick of the game and strains his ears to hear snatches of the conversation at the bar. Thomas talks to Marie, but it's hard to make out what he is saying. At best, we can get the gist from the young woman's peals of laughter. She laughs while keeping an eye on the open door, as if expecting somebody to come in.

SHE GOES OFF to look for water and meat to give the bird, while I stay behind to rummage a little in the dresser. As if the room weren't in enough of a mess already.

"Leave the door open a crack!"

What a pain he is with that megaphone! I open the door, look at them all without saying a word, and leave the door ajar. When Marie comes back with the food, I'm sitting on the bed, with my hands resting on my thighs. I stare at the parrot. I can't understand why we have to redo the whole scene . . . Our director is getting more and more het up and, I might even say, more and more confused. I look at the bird.

"He must be hungry."

"He's grown bigger . . . The cage is getting too small for him."

I stand up, stroke Marie's hair. In the corridor, I glimpse Marc as he passes holding a rifle. And then the stationmaster, heading to his room.

"He's gone to his room."

"Do you think it's the right moment?"

"Are you going or not?"

"I'm going . . ."

"Then go!"

She opens her suitcase and takes out a small photograph in a gilt frame. She looks at it. Smiles.

"Go!"

She goes. She knocks on the stationmaster's door. The director waves his arms: "Go inside!"

"Come in," says the stationmaster.

"Leave the door open," shouts the director. And the whole film crew goes inside the room to set up the camera in front of the window.

Marie has a rather strange smile. She looks younger, more heavily made-up than usual. The stationmaster seems abashed.

"How's it going?"

"All right. How about you?"

On the table is a vase of peonies. She loves their scent. She looks at the stationmaster. She goes up to him and strokes his cheeks. He doesn't flinch, turn away.

The stationmaster is silent. He strokes his chin. Marie shows him the small photograph, hands it to him with slight embarrassment.

"Here."

The stationmaster is touched. He takes the photograph, looks at it, and his forehead turns red.

"For me?"

"Yes, of course."

"Thank you. Thank you, Marie."

He is about to hug her, but the director stops him.

"Put the photograph on the table!"

"On the table?"

"On the bedside table, I mean. Quick!"

The stationmaster is genuinely touched. He looks for the right place to put the photograph. He walks toward the bedside table. But then stops.

"Is over here all right?"

Marie nods.

"How about over here?"

"Yes."

"Will over here do?"

"Yes, it will do very well!"

After that, we have to try on the dresses in my room. At intervals we caress each other, we kiss.

"Oh, this one's so pretty!"

"Yes, it is. But try that one on too. That one will definitely suit you better."

We strip naked. The parrot frets in its cage. The director is in the corridor. His instructions are getting hazier and hazier from one day to the next.

"Your tits are beautiful!"

"Not too big, are they?"

"I like them like that."

In the corridor, the stationmaster comes to a halt and watches admiringly as Marie kisses my breasts. She puts her lips around one of my nipples. She sucks greedily. And then we get dressed. We swap dresses, do each other's makeup, admire each other, laugh. The director and the stationmaster applaud.

Behind the bar, Marie looks younger than just now, in the stationmaster's room. The director doesn't know what to do to attract her attention. He argues with the cameraman, the lighting technician, everybody.

"Where's my megaphone?" he shouts.

True, his voice doesn't carry very far. What's more, if he carries on bawling like that, he'll lose his voice completely. He sees Marie talking to Thomas and seems jealous. He keeps going over to them with his light meter, to interrupt them. He's such a bore! Marie laughs at Thomas's jokes, while not forgetting to scold Marc from time to time. They're having a lot of fun. The director finds his megaphone.

"Action!"

Maybe he's jealous, this director of ours, but he also has diarrhea. There he is, perched on the toilet with his megaphone and his bottle of plonk, as if sitting on a throne.

"Carry on without me. I'll keep an eye on you from here."

And he leaves the door ajar.

Everybody laughs. How are we supposed to work in such conditions? How are we supposed to concentrate? We keep filming almost the same scenes every day . . .

"Marc, don't be stupid!"

Poor Marc. He's in a bad mood. He's sick of carrying around François's lamb. He looks at Marie with, one might say, insolence, or even exasperation. What does she want from him? He goes out the back and rids himself of the lamb by tethering it to the door. Then he goes back inside, casts a glance at Marie, and quickly climbs the stairs.

"Don't be stupid, Marc!"

The stationmaster goes upstairs behind him. Once he reaches the top of the stairs, he gets down on all fours.

"What are they getting up to up there?" asks Jean, speaking to nobody in particular.

We laugh our heads off. The director, who can't see very much from inside the toilet, shouts something unintelligible. What language is he speaking?

"Carry on," says Jeanne-Marie, assuming that this will be to the liking of the man who, seated on his throne, is emitting all kinds of shouts and groans, waving his arms and his megaphone.

Marie carries on whispering to Thomas. He tenderly takes her hand, which doesn't prevent the young woman from keeping a determined eye on the open door. What or whom is she waiting for? We hear the voice of the director, who is now invisible to most of us:

"Action!"

Quite right too. A car has just pulled up in front of the hotel. Mathieu comes in, all out of breath, and announces the arrival of the tall blond woman who follows close behind him. The woman is struggling with a large cage, within which can be seen a small eagle.

"Where is he?" asks the newcomer, and Jeanne-Marie tries to explain to her that the director is slightly indisposed.

"Indisposed?"

"Yes . . ."

Apparently, the director has not noticed this unexpected arrival.

"Action!" he shouts through the bottle instead of the megaphone, which makes his voice sound as if emanating from a great distance.

"But he's here somewhere . . . I can hear him!"

"Yes, he's here. Over there."

"Where?"

"In the toilet."

The blond woman is undaunted. She requires a signature: for the cage, for the eagle asleep behind the bars, and, of course, for the uniforms.

"What uniforms?"

"The German uniforms. Look!"

Thanks to her insistence, she finally manages to come before the director's throne. She is holding a sheaf of documents.

"What do you want?" shouts the director through his megaphone.

"A signature," answers the young woman, undaunted.

The director shows her the empty bottle and moves the megaphone aside, revealing to the young woman a smile that sooner resembles a rictus.

"Don't you want to sign?"

He ruffles what is left of his hair.

The eloquent sonority of a fart and the suffering on the director's face ought to have had some kind of effect on his interlocutor. But far from it. She is unrelenting. She hands him the documents.

"I don't need an eagle anymore," mutters the director.

"What about the uniforms?"

"Too late . . ."

"You have my every sympathy," says the woman, her voice softening. "But you might at least sign."

She gives him a fountain pen, taking the bottle from him. He studies the fountain pen, his rictus becoming more accentuated. He doesn't like this. Not one little bit!

"My guts are in turmoil," he moans.

"Come on, just one little signature . . . It won't do you any harm. Are you left-handed?"

"No, I'm not a leftist . . ."

"Then you're a man of the right . . ."

"I'm not one of them, either."

Finally, he entrusts the fountain pen to Jeanne-Marie, takes back his bottle, and lets rip with a loud fart. The continuity girl signs, since it's simpler that way, the eagle woman climbs back in her car and drives off.

We all look at the cage and the little eagle, which in the

meantime has woken up and is staring at us with round, moist eyes.

"Action!" shouts the director, but nobody moves.

The eagle attempts to spread its wings, without much success, it limps as it moves around inside the cage. And in vain does the director cry, "*mehr Licht!*" or something of the sort, since we continue to look at the eagle and the eagle looks at us, and we hear nothing more.

LEANING HIS BACK against the bar, Marc is talking to François, who keeps asking him more or less the same questions as he did a few days earlier, in one of the previous scenes. Regardless, Marc seems delighted by the conversation: he strokes the black whiskers on his chin, and then the whiskers on his cheeks and upper lip. The peasant is cradling a lamb.

"How many did you say?"

"Well, four . . . one on each side."

François takes a step backward.

"You don't say!"

"What's wrong?"

"The filthy animal. It pissed on me."

He puts the lamb on the floor. The lamb bleats.

"And how many kilometers?"

"I don't really know for sure. Let's say ten kilometers."

"That far?"

"Yes, anyway, maybe not that far. Have you never been up there?"

"Me? Why would I go? I've never needed to."

"Not for yourself . . . Don't act like you're stupid. You could have gone up there as somebody's guide, couldn't you?"

Having said that, Marc breaks off the conversation,

says, "excuse me," but instead of going to the toilet at the back, he climbs the stairs in a hurry.

"He drinks too much rotgut," says François with a grin and strokes the lamb with his boot.

A voice shouts, "Action! Back to work!"

Marc runs down the corridor, at the end of which is another toilet. He comes back out quickly, walks a few paces, gazing down at the crimson carpet. François waits for him downstairs, ready to resume their conversation. In vain! Marc is standing outside Marie's room. He hesitates, but he's never been one to hold back, to control his impulses. He presses the door handle, enters, but no sooner has he stepped inside than the two women rush at him and push him back out. They lock the door. Forlorn, he bangs his fist on the door.

The film editor takes off her glasses to wipe them.

We see the eagle in the cage. The bird seems bigger now, the cage smaller. It attempts to spread its wings.

She puts her glasses back on. Smiles contentedly.

The stationmaster walks slowly along the platform, his hands folded behind his back, deep in thought. The flag pokes from his uniform pocket. A goods train passes through the station. The stationmaster takes no notice of it.

Behind the bistro, the two women stroll with their arms around each other's waists. The cows low. A lamb gambols on the grass.

Marc runs back up the stairs. He is holding a rifle. Having reached the corridor, he slows down, comes to a halt in front of Marie's door, presses the door handle, enters.

Dressed identically, seated at a table on the grass, the

two women look at Thomas, who is opening a parcel. He pulls out a white dress. Without further ado, the women take all their clothes off, squealing in pleasure as they thank him. They pass the dress back and forth between each other, feeling the material, smelling it, before each trying it on. At Marie's insistence, Marie finally keeps the dress on.

Cut! But the voice lacks sufficient conviction.

The eagle dozes in its cage. Marc looks at it for a long moment, take a few steps backward, toward the door, slowly raises his rifle . . .

Marie is prancing around in the dress under the admiring eyes of Thomas. Jean appears in the doorway of the bistro. We hear a rifle shot. They all turn their heads.

"The bastard!"

Marie lifts up the hem of her dress and rushes into the bistro hot on the heels of Jean, who is already pounding up the stairs. The others bring up the rear.

The stationmaster is the first to reach Marie's room and feels obliged to haul Marc over the coals. Marc sits with his head bowed. The rifle is still smoking.

"What have you done?"

"Nothing. As you can see, I missed."

The stationmaster goes over to the eagle. "The poor creature!" he says and swiftly turns around: Jean, Marie, Thomas, and the other Marie burst into the room. Marie rushes at Marc, slaps him, tries to wrest the rifle away from him. The stationmaster kneels down next to the cage. He speaks without addressing anybody in particular.

"We have to release him. He's grown. He has no room inside the cage."

He looks at the windowpane that Marc's bullet has broken.

Marie shakes her head. The other Marie gives a strange smile: her face turns completely pink, as if a special spotlight were shining on her . . .

"No . . . Marie shakes her head once again."

"Yes. Better we get rid of him," says the stationmaster. "She won't be able to go up there with this bird of prey."

The other Marie merely smiles. The pink spotlight is still shining on her. Her eyes sparkle.

Marie shakes her head once more. She raises her hand to her chest.

"I don't feel well . . ."

They help her lie down on the bed.

"What's wrong with you?" asks Thomas, in alarm.

"I don't know. I'm unwell, aching all over."

Marc shows his rifle to the stationmaster and explains that even if it is old and rusty, he could have done it, all the same, he could have done it, if he had wanted to. He just wanted to issue a warning: to let them know he was there and that he was watching. That he wasn't afraid. The stationmaster regarded him with something approaching pity. The others weren't paying attention. They were busy with Marie.

"Where does it hurt?"

"Everywhere."

"A warning . . . But next time!"

The stationmaster is about to grab the gun, but the little man feints and makes a run for it.

"Bugger it!" shouts Jean, jumping up from Marie's bedside and taking three steps toward the door. He then goes back, swinging his arms.

"We should release him," says the stationmaster.

"Who?"

"The eagle. Look, the cage is too small for him. He's crammed tight . . ."

"You mean he's grown?"

"Obviously . . . We should release him!"

"But what does she think?"

Jean looks around for Marie, who has left the room.

The stationmaster shrugs. He looks at Marie. She keeps her eyes shut and her hands folded across her chest. He goes to the window.

He is only half-dressed. He rubs his arms; the morning is chilly. He seems to be waiting for something. The distant sound of an airplane.

He goes to the washbasin, looks in the mirror. He starts shaving. Painstakingly. He washes his face and neck. He gets dressed. He puts on a different pair of shoes and goes out, holding the flag.

He walks down the corridor. Comes to a halt in front of a door, listens for a few seconds, opens the door a crack: Marie is fast asleep. At the foot of the bed, the eagle dozes in its cage. Now is the moment, thinks the stationmaster and enters the room, lifts the cage, hoists it onto the windowsill. He opens the window.

The sound of the wind, wings, rustling leaves.

The stationmaster closes the door. He goes to another door and presses his ear against it. At intervals, he farts. When he finds out, he'll be pleased. But the very next moment, the stationmaster is not so sure. He scratches his nose.

The stationmaster leaves the bistro. He crosses the square. He stops to look up at the sky.

He arrives on the platform. For a long moment, he stands motionless, then he turns his head to look to his left.

Marc is there, sweeping mechanically. The stationmaster smiles. He goes up to the switchman, who seems to shrink away in fear, sweeping faster and moving away. In the doorway of the telegraph office, Thomas watches this scene with more weariness than amusement. To be more exact, he can't be bothered to make the effort to look amused.

"Any news?" asks the stationmaster, going up to him.

"News . . ."

The stationmaster turns around to look for Marc, who is no longer in sight.

"Where has he got to now?"

Always the same routine; Thomas is sick of it.

"I don't know!"

The stationmaster enters the bistro. Marie is washing the dishes.

"Why did you do it?"

The stationmaster shrugs. He does not answer straightaway. After a few seconds, he says:

"He didn't have any room. He was suffocating."

Marie smiles and looks away.

"And then Marc . . . Think about it for a moment. He's completely lost his mind because of that bird."

Mathieu comes in.

"Do you know what he's done?" asks Marie.

"The eagle . . ."

"Exactly. He opened the eagle's cage."

Mathieu says nothing. He doesn't seem particularly bothered. He sits down at a table, lights a cigarette.

"We've still got the toucan," he says.

Marie looks at him in indignation. The stationmaster grimaces and Marie can no longer help herself, she bursts out laughing.

What a bad actor she is!

"We've still got the toucan," says Mathieu.

Marie looks annoyed.

"I wonder if he's happy," says the stationmaster, with another grimace.

"Who?"

The stationmaster points his thumb at the ceiling of the bistro.

Mathieu chuckles. He looks up at the ceiling, then at the stairs, then at Marie, who is jubilant, and he says:

"Aren't we having lunch today?"

"Are you hungry?" asks Marie, trying to recompose the stern expression on her face.

"As hungry as a wolf!"

Marie pats his shoulder or simply rests her hand on it.

A man in a dressing gown quickly comes down the stairs and enters the toilet. Nobody notices him, or else they pretend not to. This bit will need to be cut . . .

Through the keyhole, Marc sees the empty cage. He goes downstairs to the bistro. He still has his rifle; he never parts with it. Mathieu, Thomas, and the stationmaster are about to eat. Marc does not look at them. He stares at Marie for a few seconds, without saying a word. He leaves the bistro by the back door.

"He's crazy, that lad!"

At the back of the bistro, Marc scans the sky. The sound of an airplane. The film editor adjusts her glasses on her nose. She takes out a handkerchief to wipe her mouth. She wipes.

It's evening and music is playing in the bistro. Mathieu drums time with his fingers on the table. François, cradling the lamb, sings horribly out of tune. Jean talks to

Thomas. Action! The voice is faint and seems to come from the toilet.

"It's quite strange all this. All of a sudden: wham!"

"That's right . . . The sky's fallen down!"

"And she was so carefree, so full of life."

"She loved to dance . . ."

"And then some!"

"She loved doing other things too . . ."

The stationmaster is playing dice.

"Your throw," he says. "What are you waiting for?"

The other player needs to go to the toilet, but it's still occupied.

"Go upstairs," advises the stationmaster.

"Why doesn't he go upstairs?"

"A question of habit, old man . . ."

At the bar, the conversation is more practical.

"We should take her to hospital. We can't leave her like this . . ."

"We can wait another two or three days. And if she doesn't get better, then obviously . . ."

"Listen, even so . . . we can't risk it. It's too dangerous. Remember the other woman?"

"Yes, that's right!"

"We need to do something. Take her to hospital."

"Yes, but how? The local train doesn't stop here anymore."

They talk quietly, making long pauses, during which they down numerous glasses of what is probably calvados. When the music stops, they can hear the conversation between Marc and François, who says:

"This morning."

Marc then asks:

"How many were there?"

"Four, including a cock."

"It's the boss's eagle!" declares Marc, without beating around the bush.

"What?"

"He opened its cage."

"You don't say!"

And François looks at the stationmaster, who imperturbably throws the dice. At the bar, Jean has just come up with a solution that the other man can't really fault.

"A stretcher?"

"Yes, a stretcher . . . It's not all that complicated. I know how, you'll see . . ."

"Leave it to me, says Marc."

With his finger François taps the barrel of Marc's gun.

"With that?"

"Yes, why not?"

Marie sees Marc showing his rifle to François, who looks at it somewhat skeptically.

"Is it loaded?"

We hear the voices of the dice players.

"Not like that. You have to shake them."

"What do you think I've been doing? Fondling them? Tell me, is that what you think?"

"Come on, throw!"

In her room, Marie is lying on the bed. The other Marie sits at her bedside. She caresses her. Marie smiles, lets her caress her.

"Does it hurt here?"

"A little."

"What about here?"

"Not so much."

"What about if you breathe?"

"But I am breathing . . ."

"If you breathe deeply . . . Breathe!"

"I am breathing."

"Harder!"

"I can't breather any harder."

"Does it hurt?"

Their whispers continue for a long time yet. On the station platform, Marc, holding his rifle, and François, cradling his lamb, cross the tracks and then enter the forest.

At the back of the bistro, Jean, Mathieu, and two peasants are putting together a stretcher. To tell the truth, it's only Jean and one of the peasants who are doing the hard work, while the others watch and make idle chatter. Jean is dissatisfied with his workmate.

"You don't even know how to hold a saw!"

"Keep your hair on."

"Never mind what they're saying, concentrate!"

"And you saw it?" Mathieu asks the other peasant, who raises his arm.

"On my life, so I did! I glimpsed it . . ."

"Over the forest?"

"Yes, it was hovering . . ."

"And you say it's bigger, a lot bigger?"

Jean stops his sawing to join in the conversation.

"But you hadn't seen it before that. How could you tell the difference?"

"True, but it was enormous!"

The sound of an airplane. They scan the cloud-covered sky. Marc raises his rifle and takes aim.

"I don't see it!" cries François.

Marc lowers his rifle. He loses his temper.

"Just leave me the hell alone, will you!"

François abruptly turns around. Marc almost drops the rifle.

"What's up?"

"Nothing. I thought I saw . . ."

"Where are you looking anyway? Stupid! Up there . . . Look, up there!"

"I don't see anything."

"Me neither. But it must be up there somewhere! Flying, hovering. It's an eagle, after all, isn't it? It's not a lion . . ."

"What do you mean, a lion?"

"I said it's not a lion."

"There aren't any . . ."

"Any what?"

The lamb bleats.

"Any lions . . ."

"Stupid!"

"It's you who's stupid! There aren't any lions around here!"

"What about toucans?"

"What about what?"

Marc makes no reply. He pricks up his ears and tightens his grip on the rifle.

"Hear that?"

"What?"

"The sound of an airplane . . ."

"Apart from that.

The two of them strain to hear. Marc rushes up to a tree. He tries to clamber up it, but can't, since the rifle encumbers him and he doesn't want to put it down. François comes up to him.

"You're scaring me."

Marc falls to one knee, takes aim, and fires. François lets go of the lamb, which bolts. Marc fires another shot.

"Are you insane? Are you trying to kill my lamb?"

He runs after the lamb on long strides. Marc looks around him, appears to panic, and runs after François, who has suddenly slowed down. Spreading his arms, François advances with bent knees: the lamb is standing at the foot of a tree. Marc carries on running, startling the lamb, which bolts yet again, running off among the trees. François runs in pursuit. In vain.

In her room, Marie gazes out of the window at a flock of sheep crossing the square. The shepherd stops for a few moments to talk to a woman holding a notebook or rather a burgundy folder.

Marie is lying stretched out on the bed.

"He oughtn't to have done such a thing . . ."

The other Marie makes no reply. Marie smiles and goes over to the bed.

"Marie!"

"How beautiful you are . . ."

"You're beautiful too."

She caresses the sick woman: her hair, her face, her neck, her chest. She places her hand on her left breast as if to feel her beating heart. Her movements are measured, almost solemn, a little too slow. She stoops to kiss her on the mouth. The woman in bed closes her eyes. She has a fever. Marie feels weary too.

"Move over a little . . ."

Now the two of them are in bed. Their eyes glitter. A voice murmurs "cut!"

On the platform, the stationmaster raises the flag and

stands motionless for a long while. Thomas comes up to him.

"Why are you still waiting?"

The stationmaster looks at him and lowers the flag.

"You're right."

Marc arrives, still holding the rifle. He has just crossed the tracks. He's wheezing like a bellows.

"I had it . . ."

"What's that you say?"

"I hit it. In the wing, up high . . ."

He lifts his arm and points at the sky, which is streaked with small clouds that have been gathering above the forested hills. The stationmaster looks without saying anything. For the irony to be even more effective, Thomas avoids taking an ironic tone of voice. He's not even surprised.

"You hit it with your blunderbuss."

"Yes, that's right!" exclaims Marc and lifts his other arm too, still holding the rifle, but pointing in the opposite direction. The stationmaster conscientiously looks in the other direction. Thomas now takes an encouraging tone of voice:

"Then he'll have fallen . . ."

"I don't know. He's probably bleeding."

"Naturally."

"He's probably bleeding, but he's big, heavily built!"

"You don't say!"

The sky grows more and more overcast. We hear the beating of wings, accompanied by the sound of an airplane. And the sound of soldiers marching through the forest.

The stretcher is almost ready.

"Will he attack large animals too?" asks Jean, straightening up, still holding a hammer. François stares at him before answering: he finds Jean's calm a little disconcerting.

"He won't dare, not yet . . ."

"He's getting bigger with each passing day, it's unheard of," says the other peasant, the one who has been slaving away next to Jean until now.

"He's growing . . ."

"Must be some gigantic species. Not native to France," says François.

"Species of what? Eagle?"

"Yes, exactly. It's not a French species. Too large, too monstrous . . ."

They all go back inside the bistro.

The film editor changes the reel. She is alone, unconcerned.

The two women are still lying on the bed. Through the open window comes the sound of an airplane.

In the bistro, Jean pours a beer. François is in the middle of a story:

". . . he knelt down and started shooting in every direction. Bang! Bang! Bang! Said there were lions . . ."

"Where?"

"Well . . . in the forest. In our forest, that's where!"

"He's a little crazy," says Jean.

"More than a little!"

"That's true. He's been like that since he did his military service."

"Right, the wee man was afraid . . ."

"Who's the wee man?"

"The lamb, I mean . . . He jumped from my arms and ran away. I couldn't catch him, the poor thing!"

"He's still in the forest, then?"

"That's right. He was terrified . . ."

Jean refills François's glass and he drinks it in one gulp. The stationmaster enters the bistro. He mutters a barely audible "hello" and climbs the stairs. He goes to his room, takes off his cap, and positions himself by the window: the village square, the station, the forest, the sky, the forest, the station again. Two men, one of whom is bald and looks like the director of photography, head for the station with two suitcases. The stationmaster smiles: they must be hoping to catch the train . . .

The stationmaster closes the window. He goes to the mirror: he has shaved this morning. There is a glimmer of excitement in his eyes, which annoys him. He needs to get a grip on himself. He bends down to pick up the book lying at the foot of the bed. He flicks through it and stops at the last or second to last page. He reads out loud in a low murmur. That blasted novella: the film editor has ended up reading it herself.

The rain will then stop, the clouds will crumble and the wind will scatter them, the sky will clear. He will rise at the break of day and his eyes will glitter with joy. In the mirror he will smile as enigmatically and intensely as the woman in the train. He will shave, put on cologne, take great care brushing his clothes, which are like new, although lately he has been wearing them every day, from off the cage he will take the red cap that is almost a shade of burgundy and he will go down to the platform. He will enter Lucas's office, look at the dusty telegraph, and then go to the window and look at the sky as it turns slightly pink above a spot known

*only to him. He will go outside, take a few steps in the
direction of the forest, listen to the leaves rustling in
waves and the cries of the birds, he will hear all the
groans and grunts and far-off shrieks rising as if from
underground or rather from the depths of the woods.
He will turn around, gaze out at the other hill, the
one in front of the station, he will look at the rusting
railway tracks, overrun with grass and weeds; he will
seat himself on the bench on the platform, and he will
wait, carefully scanning the sky.*

The hand holding the book sags and he can't repress a
shudder.

He takes a photograph from a drawer: on the terrace of
a sanatorium, a woman reads the same book the stationmaster was reading just now. Next to a deckchair, there is
a giant toucan in a cage.

She is tempted to excise this scene. But not right away,
there is all the time in the world . . .

Marc enters the bistro. Jean is behind the bar.

"A large glass!"

Jean serves him without a word. The bearded man turns
to François, who, with his back to the zinc countertop,
seems to be waiting for him to say something.

"Find it?"

"No."

"We'll go out together. Have no fear. Lions don't attack
lambs. They're too small for them. Snakes, on the other
hand . . ."

He falls silent. Jean and François stare at him in amaze
ment. Jean points a finger at his temple.

"Never mind. I'm tired," says Marc, by way of apology.

"No kidding!"

"I'm going to bed."

"Time for beddy-byes," sneers Jean.

Marc is accustomed to Jean's sarcasm. He gestures vaguely and turns his back on them. He climbs the stairs. Once he reaches the corridor, he stops, looks behind him: nobody there. He takes two strides, reaches Marie's door, listens: whispers, moans, cries of pleasure, or perhaps pain. He presses the door handle, enters the room. On the bed, the two women are locked in a passionate embrace. Marc moves closer, hypnotized.

"Beat it!" shouts Marie. "Otherwise I'll scream, I'll call the boss."

Marc leaves the room, in despair.

Another war scene, thinks the film editor, who decides to get rid of it: a sanatorium during a bombing raid, gray sky, the drone of engines, the screams of the panic-stricken patients on the grass and at the windows, waving their arms, the flames, the unbearable screams!

In the bistro they are still talking about the eagle.

"This can't go on! It's even started killing cows."

"I've seen it, seen it with my own eyes," shouts a peasant who has just come in. "It swooped down on a heifer. It was huge, huge!"

"We should call the police," suggests François.

"But how did it get to be so big?" wonders Mathieu. "It's not normal!"

"What's your definition of normal?"

"I don't really know . . ."

"Have you seen it?"

"No, I haven't . . ."

"Then why stick your oar in!" shouts François, whom nobody has ever seen so belligerent.

"I'm not sticking my oar in. What about you? Have you seen it?"

"Who, me?"

"Yes, you, bigmouth!"

"Stop your bickering," says Jean. He's kept his cool, but has to raise his voice to make himself heard.

"I've seen it," says somebody else. "With my own eyes . . ."

"I wasn't asking you," Mathieu points out, and orders himself another glass of calvados.

Another peasant arrives, all flustered. He slams the door behind him and goes to the bar, out of breath.

"I saw it, I saw it, above the forest . . ."

"Catch your breath," recommends Jean. "What did you see?"

"Come and see, it's a monster! A monster . . ."

"I'm telling you, it's not normal," says Mathieu and, having knocked back his drink, rushes to the door behind the others, who are jostling to get out. Everybody has now left, apart from Jean and Marie, who comes down the stairs and heads for the bar. She is wearing a skirt and the man's shirt we saw at the beginning of the film shoot. She goes up to Jean, behind the bar.

"How is she?" asks the barkeeper.

"Asleep."

"The stretcher is ready. We'll carry her to the hospital."

"I'm thirsty," murmurs Marie.

"Some grenadine?"

"No, a glass of water, if you please . . ."

Jean pours her a glass of water. We hear two shots being fired. And then silence. A faint, almost strangulated voice cries, "cut!" Jean turns his head: he can't see anybody. A second later, the peasants come back in, even more flustered than before. Mathieu seems to be the only one who is keeping his cool.

"Action!" The film editor lights a cigarette: it's not easy to eliminate that voice, which keeps creeping in everywhere . . .

"Unbelievable!"

"Unheard-of!"

François says to Mathieu:

"Did you see it? Did you see how big it was?"

"You'd have thought it was an airplane . . ."

"But it was an eagle!"

Marc enters, brandishing the rifle.

"I didn't miss this time!"

"Stop talking crap! We're sick of it!" says François, getting annoyed.

Marc looks at them, his eyes bulging. His face is flushed. Because he's trying to act convincing . . .

"You don't believe me? You don't believe me?"

"No," says Mathieu, with the utmost calm.

Marc isn't so easily discouraged. He gesticulates, shows them the rifle, slaps his forehead, rushes toward some imaginary point, let's say the toilet, retreats . . . Everybody laughs. The tension starts to lessen a little.

"It was above the forest . . ."

"It's true, I saw it!" somebody confirms.

"I was by the monument," says Marc.

"By the what?" interrupts Mathieu.

"In the middle of the square, I mean. And I saw it . . . I saw it . . . as clearly as I see you all now."

"All right, and then what?"

"So, I saw it, took aim . . ."

"And then you farted . . ."

"He can fart upward . . . Ha, ha, ha!"

They all clutch their sides in laughter.

"To hell with you all!"

"Shut your mouth!"

"I was trying to protect you. To hell with you! I shit on the whole lot of you . . ."

He sweeps the zinc countertop with his rifle: glasses and bottles fly every which way, breaking with a loud crash.

"Stop that, you scumbag!" shouts Mathieu, rushing to pin down the raving switchman. But he is too strong; he fights like a judoka, he wrests himself from the singer's grip, eludes the others and rushes for the exit. The door bangs behind him.

Marie picks up the broken pieces. Without saying anything. She smiles her little smile, highlighted by a beam of rosy light. She is not afraid. Not one bit.

"He's completely out of his mind," says Jean.

"We should call the police," says a peasant.

"That's right!"

"We should phone . . ."

"Jean, give me a calvados," says Mathieu.

"There aren't any glasses . . ."

"We'll drink from the bottle," somebody quips.

"I can't take any more. He killed my lamb . . ."

"Who, Marc?"

François makes no reply. Marc comes running back

in, races across the bistro, and goes out again by the back
door.

"Something needs to be done . . ."

"We'll all end up off our nuts!"

"It's a real madhouse . . ."

Behind the bar, Marie laughs softly. Everybody looks
at her. She raises her hand to her mouth, as if by way of
apology.

Once again, we hear the faint, weary voice, which, taking advantage of the moment's silence, murmurs, "cut."

The weather is fine, even if the sky is still obscured by a
thin layer of whitish cloud. Silence. Marc appears, coming
from the direction of the forest. He crosses the railroad
track. He is downcast. He walks up to the stationmaster,
who is standing motionless on the platform. The stationmaster smiles.

He is still smiling, in his room, as he stands in front of
the open window. The village square is full of people. Most
of them are crowding around a truck with a blue-green tarpaulin, which they are loading with bulky objects packed
in cardboard boxes. Marc approaches from the direction
of the station. The sky is gray.

On the television screen: images of war, refugees. These
images need to be kept, otherwise the similar images that
come before them won't make any sense. Where the hell
did he filch them all from anyway?

Marc walks up to a group of peasants, who talk among
themselves and at intervals raise their arms to point at the
sky, which is gray, dark gray. The switchman tries to join
in their conversation, even though they take no notice of
him.

"I told him: wait here another two or three days.

The police will arrive at any moment. But he was scared stiff . . ."

"Hardly surprising!"

"He was scared stiff, and if he was scared stiff . . . His wife was trembling all day long."

"All night long too?"

"All night too . . ."

"He saw it. He told me. He saw the eagle!"

"Me too," says Marc.

"He saw it," repeats the peasant.

"Then it's hardly surprising he was scared, is it?"

"Hardly surprising," says Marc.

"That's right, I'm not saying it isn't . . . But . . ."

"I'm thinking of leaving too . . ."

"What about the flock?"

"With the flock."

"We're all leaving!"

"We're leaving!"

"You cowards!" shouts Marc, but nobody pays him any mind.

"We're all getting out of here!"

"Yes!"

"No!" shouts Marc, who, by waving his rifle, finally draws attention to himself. "Listen: we have to take up arms. To resist!"

"Arms?"

"What arms?"

"Haven't you got any at home?"

"It's too big, too powerful," says François.

"We have to resist!" repeats Marc, waving his rifle.

"How?"

"We have to take up arms . . ."

"Arms?"

"If you haven't got any, then buy some . . . We need arms to defend ourselves . . ."

Where am I supposed to cut? All this shouting, all these repetitions, I'm sick and tired of it . . .

"Rabble-rouser!"

"Shut your mouth!"

"Maybe he's right . . ."

"About what?"

"We've called the police . . ."

"Rightly so," says Marc. "They have guns, the police do."

"That's just great, the police!"

"They're hardly going to arrive empty-handed."

"Let's see whether they come or not."

"Huh, the police!"

Fade to an indistinguishable clamor of voices. The stationmaster closes the window.

Marc climbs the stairs. Here he is in the corridor, still holding his rifle. He comes to a stop in front of a room, presses his ear to the door: the same whispers, the same moans, which muffle each other, cancel each other out, and finally merge in a single prolonged groan coming from the same person.

Marc looks through the keyhole: the empty cage, a leg, two legs. He does not open the door. He doesn't even attempt to open it. He doesn't dare.

The stationmaster is still in his room, in front of the closed window. He sees the police van pull up next to the crowd. Three policemen get out. He had intended to costume them as German soldiers. A good thing he thought better of it.

The peasants crowd around them. An unbelievable

commotion ensues: arms waving, fingers pointing at the sky, mouths uttering the word "eagle" (there's probably also somebody trying to shout "action" or, more likely, "cut," "it's a wrap," but who is listening?) and other words, uttered over and over again, without coalescing into any intelligible sentence . . . A policeman takes off his cap and fans himself with it, it's hot, somebody is brandishing a rifle, but for once it's not Marc, nor is it the policemen, and finally every eye fastens on the hotel sign, which grows larger and larger:

THE IMPERIAL EAGLE

Policemen and peasants cross the square. They enter the bistro.

In her room, Marie shouts, without getting out of bed: "Get out of here, you son of a bitch!"

Marc is on the other side of the door. He doesn't dare enter, but merely rattles the door handle.

"Come over here! Come see!"

François wants to show the policemen the dead animals around the back of the bistro.

We see the body of a lamb. A little way away there are others. We glimpse passing flocks as they leave the village.

The sound of an airplane. The policemen go back inside the bistro.

Marc makes his mind up. He opens the door and enters Marie's room. The two women are on the bed, one lying, the other sitting.

"Get out!"

Marie struggles to sit up in bed. Marc is transfixed by the sight of the two naked women, who are as alike as two drops of water. Or two drops of wine . . . He holds his rifle, not knowing what to do with it, he passes it from his left hand to his right and back again, staring with an inane expression on his face at Marie's huge tits, which are quivering, because she is about to yell out at the top of her voice. Recovering from his stupefaction, Marc finds nothing better to do than raise the rifle to his shoulder, while Jean, down in the bistro, refills the glasses and then freezes: we hear a gunshot.

"It's Marc," says François.

A policeman races up the stairs, followed by François and the other peasants. Marc hears footsteps in the corridor, turns around, and is about to close the door, but the policeman is too quick for him: he puts his foot in the crack and barges in with his shoulder. He bursts into the room and, before the others arrive, manages to disarm Marc, who in any event does not put up much resistance. He bundles him outside, into the corridor.

They go downstairs. Marc walks in front, with his hands up.

Marie is getting dressed. She has pulled on her old blue jeans and is now looking for her blouse. Marie, lying on the bed once more, watches her. She then closes her eyes. She looks to be in great pain.

"The Germans are here. I have to go . . ."

Marie opens her eyes.

"What Germans?"

She doesn't really understand, nor do I, but we don't say anything else about it.

In the bistro, Marc is made to answer preliminary questions. There is a commotion, a real uproar. One of the policemen examines the switchman's rifle.

"Do you have a permit for this?"

"No."

"It's an old make," says the policeman, stroking the barrel.

"From the war . . ."

"Which war?" asks François, and others echo the same question, in slightly alarmed voices.

Marc makes no reply. He sees the stationmaster coming down the stairs, without haste. He pushes his way through the crowd to Marc.

"What have you done, you wretch?"

"He's a little bit too fond of playing with his rifle," says the policeman, glaring at Marc, who looks utterly dejected; he hangs his head.

"He killed our animals!" yells a peasant.

"Who?" asks the policeman.

"He's mad!"

"A mad predator . . ."

"Why did you do it?"

Even though the policeman's voice is not particularly menacing, Marc hangs his head lower.

"Come see! It's up there, hovering . . ." shouts a peasant and rushes to the door.

"What's hovering?" asks one of the lawmen, looking around him, suddenly weary.

"Come on!"

"The eagle!"

"The eagle! The eagle!"

The peasants go outside, followed by two of the policemen. The third stays behind with the stationmaster and Jean, standing in front of Marc, who sits motionless, with his head in his hands.

Marie, now fully dressed, looks out of the window at
the square, where the peasants are pointing up at the sky,
telling the policemen to look. On the bed, Marie is asleep,
or rather she is pretending, because now she bites her lips.
Marie bends down to lift the cage, ready to put it in her
rucksack. For an instant she looks at the parrot, which
seems to have grown, but no, she says to herself, that's
ridiculous . . . And I am in complete agreement with her.

François comes back into the bistro.

"Come see!"

Marc finally agrees to answer the policeman's questions.
He waves his arms as he tells the story.

". . . then I took aim and fired. I thought I'd . . ."

The policeman interrupts.

"Yes, right . . . But tell me, what were you playing at
upstairs?"

The bearded man makes no reply. He lowers his head.
The stationmaster tries the toilet door, but it's still occupied. He shrugs and starts to climb the stairs: slowly,
slowly enough for him to be able to listen in on at least a
little more of the interrogation. But at the same time he
would like to go to Marie's room . . . In any event, there's
no reason for the camera to linger on him so long as he
slowly climbs the stairs. This needs to be cut . . .

"You were holding the rifle . . . Admit it!"

"Yes."

"In fact no, mister policeman, you can see for yourself
what an antique that rifle is," interjects François, and the
policeman casts him a glance of annoyance.

"Yes, I was, and I fired . . . Hit the target!"

So, he admits it! But the policeman is a stickler for
detail, he still has his doubts . . .

"Hit what exactly?"

"The eagle . . ."

"What eagle?" asks the policeman sourly. "Are you trying to make fun of me or what?"

"Don't lie, Marc!" says François, and the policeman stands up.

"You're having me on!"

"The policeman is going to get upset," whispers François.

Marc lowers his chin. He grips it in his hand as if he were about to rip off a mask.

"We're wasting our time. Where are the others?"

François leans over to Marc and whispers in his ear:

"Tell him the truth! It's the easiest way . . ."

"Would you like to have a drink?" Jean asks the policeman, who has come up to the bar.

"Come see, everybody!" shouts a peasant, appearing in the doorway. "It's still hovering. It hovers and hovers and then swoops to attack! It's ferocious!"

"A glass of red," requests the policeman.

Marc lifts his head.

"I'll have one too!"

"You'd be better off not drinking," recommends François.

"Why?"

More peasants enter the bistro, all of them talking at the same time.

"It's attacking in broad daylight now . . ."

"It's a ferocious beast!"

"A monster!"

"A demon!"

"A vampire!"

Look! a woman wearing jeans and carrying a rucksack slips through the crowded bistro without anybody noticing her. Nobody pays the slightest attention to her. She smiles. Before changing the reel, I need to wipe my glasses: they're steamed up. It's hot.

The stationmaster enters Marie's room without knocking.

"Oh, it's you!"

"Does it hurt?"

"Yes."

The stationmaster sits down at her bedside, strokes her hair.

"Where does it hurt?"

She takes his hand.

"Everywhere."

The sound of an airplane. She murmurs:

"You still love me . . ."

The stationmaster puts his hand on her forehead. She has a fever.

In front of the bar, Marc is feeling like himself once more; he drinks red wine and talks animatedly. Now it's the policeman's turn to look bewildered.

"It was as big as an airplane . . . hovering above the forest . . ."

"Listen," interrupts François, "you kept seeing lions . . . and snakes!"

But the switchman ignores him, doesn't listen to him, doesn't see him. He looks at the policeman. It's to the policeman that he's telling the story.

"I took aim and then, bang! Why are you laughing?"

He's now addressing the peasants. The policeman is sick of him:

"Come on, stop playing the clown!"

"Who's playing the clown?"

"You!" shouts the policeman. He's had enough. His patience has its limits . . .

"Me?"

"Are you going to tell him about the lions?" asks François.

"Lions?" yells the policeman. "You're mad! The whole lot of you!"

"I assure you, mister policeman, sir . . ."

"Cut!" shouts the policeman.

But François is in earnest, he keeps bringing up the lions because he wants to elucidate the matter. He wants to assist the agent of law and order in shedding light . . . That is what he says, emphasizing the word "light," but the policeman seems to be sick of it all, he goes to the door of the bistro, sees his car, and utters the word "action!" or else he merely thinks it: he can already imagine himself driving off . . . Outside, the other two policemen are talking.

"Let's go, we're wasting our time here," he says.

The stationmaster looks out of the window at the young woman crossing the square, heading in the direction of the station. She flits like a shadow among the peasants, scene shifters, and electricians who are loading a truck covered with a blue-green tarpaulin. A policeman comes out of the bistro, holding Marc by the arm. The peasants stop their loading, an unwonted task for them. They waver for an instant and then point up at the sky, at the eagle, which is still invisible, both to the policemen and to the viewer. To everybody, in fact. The electricians snigger. These peasants can't really . . . It must be some ritual or mania, thinks the policeman, tightly gripping the switchman's arm. Marc suddenly raises his head. The policemen can't help but raise theirs too.

"Now do you see it?"

"No, it's too cloudy . . ."

"Can't you see it? Up there, on the left, above the forest . . ."

"No, I can't see anything," says the policeman, although he can hear the sound of an airplane.

"Look at where I'm pointing," insists François.

The policeman hesitates for a moment and then, so as not to be accused of being a spoilsport, he looks over the peasant's shoulder at where he is pointing.

"Might be a plane," he mutters in the peasant's ear.

"Exactly, a plane . . ."

"I told you," cries Marc, "it's as big as a plane!"

"I can't see it anymore," says the policeman, sounding like somebody forced to play a game that is dragging on too long.

"Up there, above the forest . . ."

"I see it! I see it . . . Give me back my rifle!"

"You're getting on my nerves . . ."

"My rifle! I'll shoot it down, you'll see . . ."

Marc breaks free of the policeman's grip and aims an imaginary rifle at the sky.

"Boom! Boom!"

"Stop it!" shouts François. "We've had enough of your playacting."

"Watch it!" says the policeman, losing his temper. "Or else I'll put the cuffs on you."

"The cuffs, but why?"

"You'll see . . ."

"But I didn't do anything!"

François tries to calm things down. He weighs his words carefully.

"Listen . . . Don't go over the top . . ."

"What did you say?" barks the policeman, who has a hard time admitting to himself that he has lost control of the situation. He therefore gets on his high horse. But François won't back down, he's not afraid to repeat his words.

"Don't go over the top . . . He may be crazy, he may be a clown, but he hasn't done anything. Apart from telling tall tales. That's all. Don't you understand?"

"Understand what?"

"That he's a braggart."

"Who, me?" bristles Marc.

"Yes, he's right," interjects Mathieu. "He hasn't killed anybody."

A flock of sheep crosses the square, and then an old banger laden with luggage. The family of the peasant behind the wheel follow on foot.

"Leaving?"

"Yes, we are."

"What's got into you all? Have you all gone mad?" asks the policeman in desperation, waving Marc's rifle.

"It's because you're not up to the job of protecting us . . ." says François, philosophically.

"Give me back my rifle," groans Marc.

Behind the bistro, Jean and Thomas gaze at the stretcher, which is now ready.

"Do you think it will hold?"

"Yes, no doubt about it."

In the field can be seen the dead body of a cow.

Jean looks at the sky. Thomas lifts his arm to point at something.

"It's only a plane . . ."

"Maybe . . ."

The policemen climb back into their van. They have confiscated the rifle, given that its supposed owner, unable to produce a permit, has been acting in a manner dangerous to the community. The police report is stern and the party concerned ought to be thankful to have got off so lightly . . . But Marc is having none of it. He wants his gun back.

"I need it. It's dangerous around here . . ."

"You must be joking . . ."

"Give him back his gun," says François, walking up to the police van. But it speeds off.

"Bastards!"

"Cowards!"

"Call that a police force?"

"Shame on them!"

Marc tosses stones at the police van, which departs at high speed. The sound of jeers and whistles. A troop train passes through the station. I let it pass. I'm not going to cut anything else. More bands of peasants and their flocks leave the village. The truck with the blue-green tarpaulin is also about to leave. At his window, or rather at Marie's window, the stationmaster waves his flag, or else it is a red scarf, or a handkerchief.

We now see Thomas sitting at Marie's bedside.

"We'll set out tomorrow."

"For the sanatorium?" There is a slight quaver in Marie's voice.

"We'll telephone ahead to let them know."

"They're all leaving," says the stationmaster in a grave

voice. He is troubled, almost overwrought. Unless he is pretending. You never know with him . . .

"Of course they're leaving. They're scared out of their wits," adds Thomas.

"It's a real exodus," says the stationmaster.

It's completely slapdash and there's nothing more I can do with it . . . I wipe my glasses, light a cigarette. I'm tired.

"I'm not afraid."

Marie tightly grips Thomas's arm. She's not very convincing.

"Calm down," says Thomas. "It will all be over tomorrow morning . . ."

"What will be over?"

"I mean, we'll be leaving . . . I'm sick of it all too."

"Where is he now?"

Thomas makes no reply. He doesn't know. He looks at the stationmaster, who doesn't feel obliged to say anything. He's not responsible for it . . .

The door opens. Slowly, very slowly. We see Marc's head. He looks at Marie, at her alone.

"Marie . . ."

"Come in, if you like, but close the door. There's a draft," says the stationmaster.

But Marc prefers to go away.

At the window once more, the stationmaster gazes at the russet sky, at the sun setting behind the forest.

"The weather will be fine tomorrow," he prophesies. He makes no attempt to conceal his satisfaction. And he carries on looking at the forest, the station, the square without the monument, the peasants . . . There are fewer and fewer of them, they're all leaving! Where will this rural

exodus leave us? The last of the flocks depart. Cars, bicy-
cles . . . We hear the sound of the helicopter from which
all these scenes are being filmed, and still I don't make
any cuts.

The plain is littered with carcasses: calves, cows, pigs,
chickens. Jean, Thomas, and Mathieu come for the
stretcher, which they have left propped against the honeysuckle hedge. Is that the sound of an airplane or a helicopter? In any event, the difference is imperceptible to the
untrained ear. They pause for a moment, lift their heads,
look at the sky, which is clearer than it has been the last
few days. But it is still cloudy . . .

ALONG THE CORRIDOR of a hotel, a woman is being borne carefully along on a stretcher by four men, one of whom, shorter than the others, has a black beard and rather slanted eyes. Because he is so short, the others have to forgo holding the shafts at arm's length and, for the same reason, he has to refrain from resting the wooden handle on his shoulder: his exertion is therefore greater, although he is quite brawny . . .

"Look out!"

"Stop! Okay, it's all right now . . ."

"Let's go!"

"Marie," says the short man, but he doesn't dare turn his head.

"Yes, Marc."

"How are you feeling?"

"I'm fine . . ."

"Mind the stairs!"

"Easy does it!"

"Not so fast," demands a character wearing a brand-new stationmaster's uniform, who accompanies the stretcher bearers and supervises them as they descend the stairs.

"Open the door, Mathieu!"

"Never mind, I'll open it . . ."

The stationmaster overtakes the stretcher bearers,

brushing past the bar, and opens wide the double door
to the bistro. He then takes a step back and waits as the
stretcher bearers go out. His face betrays an excitement
that might equally be read as joy or as anguish. He turns
his head. There must be somebody inside the toilet to the
left of the staircase: the thuds of somebody knocking on
the inside of the door can be heard, and a slow whining,
like a broken siren. The stationmaster shrugs. The others
pay no attention.

The stretcher bearers cross the square. The man in uniform walks alongside them, holding his hands behind his
back. We see them nearing the station. The sky is overcast, but it isn't raining. They are now shown to us from
closer up, on the platform. The stretcher bearers hesitate
for a moment, before crossing the tracks. They enter the
forest. The sound of rustling leaves and dry twigs cracking
beneath their feet is louder than the twittering of the birds.

I don't understand any of this. I should have got here at
the beginning of the film, like everybody else . . .

The woman on the stretcher has her eyes closed, she
seems to be asleep. She still has her eyes closed as she now
lies on a chaise longue on the terrace of a sanatorium, but
maybe she isn't asleep, maybe she is lying in wait or merely
watching through her long eyelashes, which quiver imperceptibly: maybe she is watching the other patients on the
other chaises longues, as the nurses move among them,
murmuring unintelligible words, probably in German or
Russian . . . What kind of a film is this?

She lies in wait, listens. A huge shadow falls over the
scene.

Four men are carrying a stretcher. Another man stands
to the side, at the bottom of a tree. No, he's not taking a

leak, he's looking up at the sky, or at what can be seen of it through the canopy of leaves.

On a television screen I see an eagle in flight: wings outspread, it hovers. There is nobody sitting in front of the television set, which goes to show that, in the director's mind, television can function perfectly well without any viewers . . .

I turn my head just as somebody stands up and walks out of the cinema auditorium. I resist the temptation to follow his example, or even to get up and go to the john.

The group comes to a stop in a small glade. They place the stretcher on the ground. Marc tends to Marie, caresses her tenderly.

"How do you feel?"

Marie makes no reply. She looks at the others, who are talking among themselves in a low voices, making her strain her ears to hear what they are saying. She makes a sign for Marc to be quiet.

"It's stupid!"

"But even so, I'm going back . . . I have to go back!"

"Do what you think is best . . ."

"I'm going back, Jean. There's nothing else I can do."

The stationmaster's voice is calm and determined. But Jean feels obliged to try to persuade him one last time.

"Listen, boss, it's stupid. The local train won't be stopping at the station anymore. Is it or isn't it true?" He is now speaking to the character with long blond hair, whose name is Thomas or Lucas.

"Yes, it's true," he replies.

"It won't be stopping anymore. The station has been taken off the route. Think about it for a moment."

"I have to go back . . ."

"Let him go. He knows better than we do what he has to do," says Lucas. Or rather Thomas.

"He's right," interjects the fourth man, whose name seems to be Mathieu.

"Who?"

"Thomas . . ."

They all fall silent. They look at Marie, who moves her lips without making a sound. Her gaze is elsewhere, she is looking into empty space, she scratches her arm mechanically. Marc leaves the path and walks a few yards away. The stationmaster takes a wad of banknotes from his jacket pocket.

"Take this!"

"What about you?" asks Jean, taking the money.

"I've kept a little for myself."

"Let's go, it's getting late," says Thomas.

The stationmaster goes up to the stretcher. For a few seconds, he stands motionless next to Marie, who now has her eyes closed, although she's definitely not asleep. He doesn't think to kneel down and kiss her. But he bows his head, until his chin touches the knot of his necktie.

"Farewell, Marie," says the stationmaster.

Marie opens her eyes at last, looks at him without saying anything.

"Let's go," says Thomas.

The four men lift the stretcher, rest it on their shoulders, and set off again.

"Goodbye, old man!" says Marc, turning his head, causing the others to cavil, because even as it is, the stretcher is sagging a little too much on his side.

The stationmaster remains rooted to the spot, watching as they move into the distance. He is not sad. Not at all.

He turns around, walks back the way he came, with a sure but rather stiff gait. His face is more relaxed than it was before. He walks with a definite aim.

He emerges from the forest, crosses the tracks. He trips against a stone, loses his balance, but does not fall. He continues on his way.

The stationmaster crosses the empty square. The body of a lamb lies in the middle of the square, in the spot where . . . He comes to a halt, studies the lifeless body, and then lifts his eyes to look at the hotel sign.

THE IMPERIAL EAGLE

The sound of an airplane. A shadow moves across the screen. Somebody else getting up to leave or to go to the toilet: as if he had a sudden craving for reality, for what is known as reality due to our constantly going through the same motions day after day after day. Once behind the metal partition, he takes out his dick and looks up at the cracked wall, the ventilation duct . . . It's comforting! He washes his hands, lights a cigarette. The woman on my right scratches her arm. The man to my right seems to have dozed off. Folded across his chest, his hands rise and fall rhythmically.

Whereas the stationmaster, lying in bed, sooner seems to be waiting, with his eyes wide open. On the bedside table, sundry items: a button, a whistle, an alarm clock, against which is propped a photograph. We are shown the photograph for a long moment. It grows larger and larger, until finally it fills the whole screen, with the ticking of the alarm clock becoming louder and louder all the while.

The stationmaster now stands in front of the window,

in his long johns and undervest. He looks out at the small square, the station, the wooded hills, the overcast sky.

He starts to do some exercises: he inhales sufficient air to inflate his rather puny rib cage, he spreads his arms, bends forward, and tries to touch his toes with his fingertips. He is far from being able to perform these rather basic exercises, but it doesn't stop him from trying. Naturally, under the circumstances, the time passes slowly . . .

The stationmaster goes to the mirror above the washbasin, studies himself with satisfaction. I cast a glance at the man sitting next to me, who has just woken up. He turns his head and gives me a conspiratorial smile. Why? The stationmaster brushes his teeth, gargles, spits noisily. He grimaces. He has a toothache. The woman behind me bursts out laughing.

The body of the lamb, lying in the rain. The man stands by the window, he takes a bite of a brioche and masticates vigorously. Having finished eating, he gets dressed: a white shirt, a well-pressed uniform. In front of the mirror, he knots his necktie, which is red, the same as his cap. He seems satisfied, happy even. He rubs the wings of his nose until they turn crimson. He sits down in an armchair, holding a book. But he does not read. He sits motionless in the armchair for a long moment. He looks at the photograph on the bedside table: it shows the woman whom we saw lying on the stretcher a little earlier. Except she is younger . . .

The stationmaster goes back to the window: it is no longer raining.

He sits back down in the armchair. He stares into space, in other words, he peers into the cinema auditorium, gazes at us. His eyes are tranquil. The man next to me yawns.

The stationmaster is asleep. Maybe he is not asleep, but pretending. I place my hand on the arm of the woman next to me, I wait, she makes no reaction. I withdraw my hand. We now see the bed, the body stretched out on the bed, the hands folded on top of the rose-madder coverlet. The bare wall.

The man's eyes are now wide open, he moves them from right to left, as if looking for something, some object he requires. On the bedside table there is a photograph. I don't know why, but I get the impression that the woman in the photograph looks like the woman sitting next to me. I look at her, it's quite hard to make out her face, I'll have to wait till the end of the film to be certain.

The stationmaster gets up from the bed, goes to the window: it's raining.

He goes to the washbasin, starts shaving, lathers his face with too much shaving cream. Must be his idea of fun . . .

He gets dressed. He knots his necktie, which is red, the same as the flag poking from an empty calvados bottle. He sits down in the armchair. He looks at the photograph of Marie. The woman sitting next to me also seems to be fascinated by the woman in the photograph, whose rather ordinary beauty only reinforces my conviction that the two of them look alike.

It is no longer raining. The sky starts to clear.

The stationmaster stands up, opens the cupboard, rummages for a few moments, goes back to his armchair, holding an album. The album is thick, bound in shagreen, like the one I saw a few days ago at the house of a friend who's a casting agent. He strokes the cover. Hesitates before opening it.

The first photograph is very yellowed. It is a wedding

photograph, in which with difficulty you can make out the face of a woman who must be Marie. The groom is the stationmaster. We then see the same people walking along the station platform, then in front of a clump of peonies that partly obscures a low building, probably a storeroom. In those days, the station was more splendid. Or more likely, it's not the same station!

Behind the inn, the wedding feast is being held amid gaiety and in an idyllic setting. A little way away, on the grass, we see cows and sheep grazing. Among the wedding guests, only the bearded man is not to be seen.

The stationmaster stands up, goes to the window: the sky is growing clearer. He smiles, goes to the mirror, straightens his tie knot, rubs his nose, returns to the album, which he opens at random.

Jean is busy behind the bar. It must be downstairs, in the bistro, because I recognize the staircase. And then a young man who looks like Marc, in military uniform, without the beard. A singer, also in the bistro, accompanied by an accordionist. Thomas and Marie dance. He clasps her waist very tightly, she smiles. The stationmaster plays dice. Marie serves two soldiers at the bar. We can't see the soldiers' faces. From their uniforms, they might be Russian, it's not impossible, but I can't be sure of it . . .

The stationmaster flicks through the album more quickly. He pauses for a moment on a photograph of an extremely young Marie, so young that you might think it's another woman, or sooner a young girl who resembles her. I look at the woman next to me, who is leaning forward, resting her chin on the back of the seat in front.

Marc in a private's uniform once again. And then a postcard, showing a lion hunt. It's a bad reproduction, because the lion looks more like a lemon smeared with marmalade. The woman next to me chuckles, turns her head and flashes me a smile that melts my heart. But I didn't even say anything to her! On the terrace of a sanatorium, Marie sits on a chaise longue, smiling almost the same smile. Next to her is a parrot or rather a toucan that is striking for its unusually large size and vivid plumage.

We see another train packed with soldiers armed to the teeth, a snake at the foot of a tree, probably an apple tree, a peasant cradling a lamb, whose fleece is stained with wine, and in the background, barely visible, a man in a short-sleeved shirt holding a megaphone to his mouth. All these disparate photographs are boring me senseless . . . Maybe I should have watched the whole film from the very beginning to be able to understand it? But what is there to understand?

The stationmaster puts the album on the table and feverishly picks up a book with a white and blue-green cover. It's easier when you're reading a book: you can go back to it whenever you like, skip the boring bits, the descriptions, for example . . . Or you can read the ending first, the last page, like the character in the film: he looks as impatient as a reader who wants to find out what happens at the end of the story.

There, above the forest, the sky will continue to change color: it will gradually turn from pink to red, and then a brighter, stronger red, a crimson red, an imperial red! And then all the sounds of the forest will fall silent, the only thing to be heard will be the flapping of the gigantic eagle's silver wings, as it bursts from the tree canopy, growing vast, darkening the hills and woods

*with its shadow, and it will fly higher, ever higher,
gleaming silver against the crimson silk of the sky, it will
wheel, once, twice, countless times, first soaring, then
swooping, and it will wheel ever more slowly, above the
railway station, above your head, your face transfigured
with emotion, your eyes moist with joy, your throat dry,
your muscles aching as you crane your neck to watch the
ever broader, ever lower circles that the eagle traces in
the sky, and finally, a shadow will darken all, you will
start to unbutton your uniform, your shirt, as the eagle
flies nearer and nearer, lower and lower, as its wings
thrum, rocking the sky, as the branches of the trees toss,
as the oak bends to the ground, as the station roof is torn
off in the gust, shadow and cold, the silver wings ever
closer, ever closer: you no longer see the sky, the eagle is
now your sky . . .*

The stationmaster stands up and, stuffing the book
in his pocket, he once more goes to the window. But he
does not linger there long, he goes to the mirror above the
washbasin and then to the cupboard, which is still open.
With his knee he closes one of the doors and goes back to
his armchair: in passing, he picks up the album, opens it at
a photograph, in which, behind Marie's chaise longue, we
notice another woman, who bears a perfect resemblance
to her. She is standing between Marc and Thomas. Marc,
in soldier's uniform, is unshaven. We can make out a scar
on his cheek.

He closes the album, tries to look out of the window,
without getting up out of the armchair. He opens the
album once more: behind the inn, lots of people sit around

a table on which a lamb is perched. In the sunlight, it is as if the lamb itself radiates light, as if it shines.

The stationmaster puts the album on the table, next to the bottle of calvados.

The sky is almost blue.

The stationmaster leaves the room. He walks down the corridor in long strides.

"*Merde!*"

He says "*merde*" because he trips on the threadbare carpet, totters, almost loses his balance. The woman next to me laughs. Still laughing, she resumes a normal sitting position. I feel her arm next to mine on the armrest. The man on my right sits up straight, stretches his arms, without caring that he is blocking my view, yawns, stands up, and leaves. Other filmgoers do likewise.

The stationmaster now descends the stairs cautiously, even hesitantly. At the bottom of the stairs, he looks around the empty room, the empty bistro, I mean, and turns left to go to the toilet. He opens the toilet door and peers inside, as if he were looking for someone. But there is nobody there. He shakes his head and goes to the door that gives onto the field littered with animal carcasses. We also notice an abandoned car, turned on its side.

The stationmaster walks over the grass for a few paces. He takes a deep breath.

The sky is almost blue.

The cinema is empty. On the bedside table, the photograph of Marie. We hear the ticking of the alarm clock. We see the wall, the window, the album on the table, next to the flag.

Here is the stationmaster. He enters. He goes to the

window. He looks at the square, the station, the wooded hills. The sound of an airplane, he turns around, goes to the table, takes the flag, and leaves the room.

In the corridor, he comes to a stop in front of a door. He listens, opens the door a crack: an unmade bed, a woman's underwear. He closes the door, continues along the corridor, but he seems undecided, he comes to a stop in front of another door, crouches down, looks through the keyhole, sees nothing: a blank wall.

He goes downstairs. He turns his head, glances behind him: nobody. Alone at last . . . He inserts his index finger in one nostril to excavate some mucus. He carefully picks his nose.

He crosses the square, dragging his feet, stops in front of a dead lamb. Even the woman who had been sitting next to me has left. The cinema is emptying. Maybe there's nobody here but me. I ask myself why I don't leave. What am I waiting for?

He walks along the station platform, holding his flag. The sound of an airplane, now much louder. But I can't see anything, which is to say, the sky is empty, blue, clear. If you look down, the railroad tracks are overrun with weeds. All the way into the distance, out of sight. The stationmaster stands motionless for a long time. And then he raises his flag to salute an invisible train. The train passes very, very slowly, or else it comes to a halt in the little station. I feel a tingling in my arms and legs. Abruptly, he turns on his heel and heads toward the telegraph office. He enters but comes straight back out again. He walks onto the platform and looks right and left. I do likewise. I stand up. The forest is all aflutter: the rustle of leaves, the snuffling of small creatures seeking shelter. I dare not budge. The sky is blue, dazzling. My eyes hurt. I clench my eyelids and stand motionless. There is no further sound. And I'm waiting, still waiting, my eyes closed, unaware that the lights have come up in the cinema auditorium.

I place my hand on the backs of the seats to steady myself as I walk up the aisle. I stagger, staring at the red carpet, worn bare by the shuffling soles of so many film-goers. I raise my head, and there, at last, smiling, holding her usherette's torch, Marie points me to the exit.

MICHAL AJVAZ, *The Golden Age.*
The Other City.

PIERRE ALBERT-BIROT, *Grabinoulor.*

YUZ ALESHKOVSKY, *Kangaroo.*

FELIPE ALFAU, *Chromos.*
Locos.

JOE AMATO, *Samuel Taylor's Last Night.*

IVAN ÂNGELO, *The Celebration.*
The Tower of Glass.

ANTÓNIO LOBO ANTUNES, *Knowledge of Hell.*
The Splendor of Portugal.

ALAIN ARIAS-MISSON, *Theatre of Incest.*

JOHN ASHBERY & JAMES SCHUYLER, *A Nest of Ninnies.*

ROBERT ASHLEY, *Perfect Lives.*

GABRIELA AVIGUR-ROTEM, *Heatwave and Crazy Birds.*

DJUNA BARNES, *Ladies Almanack.*
Ryder.

JOHN BARTH, *Letters.*
Sabbatical.

DONALD BARTHELME, *The King.*
Paradise.

SVETISLAV BASARA, *Chinese Letter.*

MIQUEL BAUÇÀ, *The Siege in the Room.*

RENÉ BELLETTO, *Dying.*

MAREK BIENCZYK, *Transparency.*

ANDREI BITOV, *Pushkin House.*

ANDREJ BLATNIK, *You Do Understand.*
Law of Desire.

LOUIS PAUL BOON, *Chapel Road.*
My Little War.
Summer in Termuren.

ROGER BOYLAN, *Killoyle.*

IGNÁCIO DE LOYOLA BRANDÃO, *Anonymous Celebrity.*
Zero.

BONNIE BREMSER, *Troia: Mexican Memoirs.*

CHRISTINE BROOKE-ROSE, *Amalgamemnon.*

BRIGID BROPHY, *In Transit.*
The Prancing Novelist.

GERALD L. BRUNS, *Modern Poetry and the Idea of Language.*

GABRIELLE BURTON, *Heartbreak Hotel.*

MICHEL BUTOR, *Degrees.*
Mobile.

G. CABRERA INFANTE, *Infante's Inferno.*
Three Trapped Tigers.

JULIETA CAMPOS, *The Fear of Losing Eurydice.*

ANNE CARSON, *Eros the Bittersweet.*

ORLY CASTEL-BLOOM, *Dolly City.*

LOUIS-FERDINAND CÉLINE, *North.*
Conversations with Professor Y.
London Bridge.

MARIE CHAIX, *The Laurels of Lake Constance.*

HUGO CHARTERIS, *The Tide Is Right.*

ERIC CHEVILLARD, *Demolishing Nisard.*
The Author and Me.

MARC CHOLODENKO, *Mordechai Schamz.*

JOSHUA COHEN, *Witz.*

EMILY HOLMES COLEMAN, *The Shutter of Snow.*

ERIC CHEVILLARD, *The Author and Me.*

ROBERT COOVER, *A Night at the Movies.*

STANLEY CRAWFORD, *Log of the S.S. The Mrs Unguentine.*
Some Instructions to My Wife.

RENÉ CREVEL, *Putting My Foot in It.*

RALPH CUSACK, *Cadenza.*

NICHOLAS DELBANCO, *Sherbrookes.*
The Count of Concord.

NIGEL DENNIS, *Cards of Identity.*

PETER DIMOCK, *A Short Rhetoric for Leaving the Family.*

ARIEL DORFMAN, *Konfidenz.*

COLEMAN DOWELL, *Island People.*
Too Much Flesh and Jabez.

ARKADII DRAGOMOSHCHENKO, *Dust.*

RIKKI DUCORNET, *Phosphor in Dreamland.*
The Complete Butcher's Tales.

RIKKI DUCORNET (cont.), *The Jade Cabinet*.
The Fountains of Neptune.

WILLIAM EASTLAKE, *The Bamboo Bed*.
Castle Keep.
Lyric of the Circle Heart.

JEAN ECHENOZ, *Chopin's Move*.

STANLEY ELKIN, *A Bad Man*.
Criers and Kibitzers, Kibitzers and Criers.
The Dick Gibson Show.
The Franchiser.
The Living End.
Mrs. Ted Bliss.

FRANÇOIS EMMANUEL, *Invitation to a Voyage*.

PAUL EMOND, *The Dance of a Sham*.

SALVADOR ESPRIU, *Ariadne in the Grotesque Labyrinth*.

LESLIE A. FIEDLER, *Love and Death in the American Novel*.

JUAN FILLOY, *Op Oloop*.

ANDY FITCH, *Pop Poetics*.

GUSTAVE FLAUBERT, *Bouvard and Pécuchet*.

KASS FLEISHER, *Talking out of School*.

JON FOSSE, *Aliss at the Fire*.
Melancholy.

FORD MADOX FORD, *The March of Literature*.

MAX FRISCH, *I'm Not Stiller*.
Man in the Holocene.

CARLOS FUENTES, *Christopher Unborn*.
Distant Relations.
Terra Nostra.
Where the Air Is Clear.

TAKEHIKO FUKUNAGA, *Flowers of Grass*.

WILLIAM GADDIS, JR., *The Recognitions*.

JANICE GALLOWAY, *Foreign Parts*.
The Trick Is to Keep Breathing.

WILLIAM H. GASS, *Life Sentences*.
The Tunnel.
The World Within the Word.
Willie Masters' Lonesome Wife.

GÉRARD GAVARRY, *Hoppla! 1 2 3*.

ETIENNE GILSON, *The Arts of the Beautiful*.
Forms and Substances in the Arts.

C. S. GISCOMBE, *Giscome Road*.
Here.

DOUGLAS GLOVER, *Bad News of the Heart*.

WITOLD GOMBROWICZ, *A Kind of Testament*.

PAULO EMÍLIO SALES GOMES, *P's Three Women*.

GEORGI GOSPODINOV, *Natural Novel*.

JUAN GOYTISOLO, *Count Julian*.
Juan the Landless.
Makbara.
Marks of Identity.

HENRY GREEN, *Blindness*.
Concluding.
Doting.
Nothing.

JACK GREEN, *Fire the Bastards!*

JIŘÍ GRUŠA, *The Questionnaire*.

MELA HARTWIG, *Am I a Redundant Human Being?*

JOHN HAWKES, *The Passion Artist*.
Whistlejacket.

ELIZABETH HEIGHWAY, ED., *Contemporary Georgian Fiction*.

AIDAN HIGGINS, *Balcony of Europe*.
Blind Man's Bluff.
Bornholm Night-Ferry.
Langrishe, Go Down.
Scenes from a Receding Past.

KEIZO HINO, *Isle of Dreams*.

KAZUSHI HOSAKA, *Plainsong*.

ALDOUS HUXLEY, *Antic Hay*.
Point Counter Point.
Those Barren Leaves.
Time Must Have a Stop.

NAOYUKI II, *The Shadow of a Blue Cat*.

DRAGO JANČAR, *The Tree with No Name*.

MIKHEIL JAVAKHISHVILI, *Kvachi*.

GERT JONKE, *The Distant Sound*.
Homage to Czerny.
The System of Vienna.

SELECTED DALKEY ARCHIVE TITLES

JACQUES JOUET, *Mountain R.*
Savage.
Upstaged.
MIEKO KANAI, *The Word Book.*
YORAM KANIUK, *Life on Sandpaper.*
ZURAB KARUMIDZE, *Dagny.*
JOHN KELLY, *From Out of the City.*
HUGH KENNER, *Flaubert, Joyce and Beckett: The Stoic Comedians.*
Joyce's Voices.
DANILO KIŠ, *The Attic.*
The Lute and the Scars.
Psalm 44.
A Tomb for Boris Davidovich.
ANITA KONKKA, *A Fool's Paradise.*
GEORGE KONRÁD, *The City Builder.*
TADEUSZ KONWICKI, *A Minor Apocalypse.*
The Polish Complex.
ANNA KORDZAIA-SAMADASHVILI, *Me, Margarita.*
MENIS KOUMANDAREAS, *Koula.*
ELAINE KRAF, *The Princess of 72nd Street.*
JIM KRUSOE, *Iceland.*
AYSE KULIN, *Farewell: A Mansion in Occupied Istanbul.*
EMILIO LASCANO TEGUI, *On Elegance While Sleeping.*
ERIC LAURRENT, *Do Not Touch.*
VIOLETTE LEDUC, *La Bâtarde.*
EDOUARD LEVÉ, *Autoportrait.*
Newspaper.
Suicide.
Works.
MARIO LEVI, *Istanbul Was a Fairy Tale.*
DEBORAH LEVY, *Billy and Girl.*
JOSÉ LEZAMA LIMA, *Paradiso.*
ROSA LIKSOM, *Dark Paradise.*
OSMAN LINS, *Avalovara.*
The Queen of the Prisons of Greece.
FLORIAN LIPUŠ, *The Errors of Young Tjaž.*
GORDON LISH, *Peru.*
ALF MACLOCHLAINN, *Out of Focus.*
Past Habitual.

The Corpus in the Library.
RON LOEWINSOHN, *Magnetic Field(s).*
YURI LOTMAN, *Non-Memoirs.*
D. KEITH MANO, *Take Five.*
MINA LOY, *Stories and Essays of Mina Loy.*
MICHELINE AHARONIAN MARCOM, *A Brief History of Yes.*
The Mirror in the Well.
BEN MARCUS, *The Age of Wire and String.*
WALLACE MARKFIELD, *Teitlebaum's Window.*
DAVID MARKSON, *Reader's Block.*
Wittgenstein's Mistress.
CAROLE MASO, *AVA.*
HISAKI MATSUURA, *Triangle.*
LADISLAV MATEJKA & KRYSTYNA POMORSKA, EDS., *Readings in Russian Poetics: Formalist & Structuralist Views.*
HARRY MATHEWS, *Cigarettes.*
The Conversions.
The Human Country.
The Journalist.
My Life in CIA.
Singular Pleasures.
The Sinking of the Odradek.
Stadium.
Tlooth.
HISAKI MATSUURA, *Triangle.*
DONAL MCLAUGHLIN, *beheading the virgin mary, and other stories.*
JOSEPH MCELROY, *Night Soul and Other Stories.*
ABDELWAHAB MEDDEB, *Talismano.*
GERHARD MEIER, *Isle of the Dead.*
HERMAN MELVILLE, *The Confidence-Man.*
AMANDA MICHALOPOULOU, *I'd Like.*
STEVEN MILLHAUSER, *The Barnum Museum.*
In the Penny Arcade.
RALPH J. MILLS, JR., *Essays on Poetry.*
MOMUS, *The Book of Jokes.*
CHRISTINE MONTALBETTI, *The Origin of Man.*
Western.

NICHOLAS MOSLEY, *Accident.*
Assassins.
Catastrophe Practice.
A Garden of Trees.
Hopeful Monsters.
Imago Bird.
Inventing God.
Look at the Dark.
Metamorphosis.
Natalie Natalia.
Serpent.

WARREN MOTTE, *Fables of the Novel:*
French Fiction since 1990.
Fiction Now: The French Novel in the
21st Century.
Mirror Gazing.
Oulipo: A Primer of Potential Literature.

GERALD MURNANE, *Barley Patch.*
Inland.

YVES NAVARRE, *Our Share of Time.*
Sweet Tooth.

DOROTHY NELSON, *In Night's City.*
Tar and Feathers.

ESHKOL NEVO, *Homesick.*

WILFRIDO D. NOLLEDO, *But for*
the Lovers.

BORIS A. NOVAK, *The Master of*
Insomnia.

FLANN O'BRIEN, *At Swim-Two-Birds.*
The Best of Myles.
The Dalkey Archive.
The Hard Life.
The Poor Mouth.
The Third Policeman.

CLAUDE OLLIER, *The Mise-en-Scène.*
Wert and the Life Without End.

PATRIK OUŘEDNÍK, *Europeana.*
The Opportune Moment, 1855.

BORIS PAHOR, *Necropolis.*

FERNANDO DEL PASO, *News from*
the Empire.
Palinuro of Mexico.

ROBERT PINGET, *The Inquisitory.*
Mahu or The Material.
Trio.

MANUEL PUIG, *Betrayed by Rita*
Hayworth.

The Buenos Aires Affair.
Heartbreak Tango.

RAYMOND QUENEAU, *The Last Days.*
Odile.
Pierrot Mon Ami.
Saint Glinglin.

ANN QUIN, *Berg.*
Passages.
Three.
Tripticks.

ISHMAEL REED, *The Free-Lance*
Pallbearers.
The Last Days of Louisiana Red.
Ishmael Reed: The Plays.
Juice!
The Terrible Threes.
The Terrible Twos.
Yellow Back Radio Broke-Down.

JASIA REICHARDT, *15 Journeys Warsaw*
to London.

JOÃO UBALDO RIBEIRO, *House of the*
Fortunate Buddhas.

JEAN RICARDOU, *Place Names.*

RAINER MARIA RILKE,
The Notebooks of Malte Laurids Brigge.

JULIÁN RÍOS, *The House of Ulysses.*
Larva: A Midsummer Night's Babel.
Poundemonium.

ALAIN ROBBE-GRILLET, *Project for a*
Revolution in New York.
A Sentimental Novel.

AUGUSTO ROA BASTOS, *I the Supreme.*

DANIËL ROBBERECHTS, *Arriving in*
Avignon.

JEAN ROLIN, *The Explosion of the*
Radiator Hose.

OLIVIER ROLIN, *Hotel Crystal.*

ALIX CLEO ROUBAUD, *Alix's Journal.*

JACQUES ROUBAUD, *The Form of*
a City Changes Faster, Alas, Than the
Human Heart.
The Great Fire of London.
Hortense in Exile.
Hortense Is Abducted.
Mathematics: The Plurality of Worlds of
Lewis.
Some Thing Black.

RAYMOND ROUSSEL, *Impressions of Africa.*

VEDRANA RUDAN, *Night.*

PABLO M. RUIZ, *Four Cold Chapters on the Possibility of Literature.*

GERMAN SADULAEV, *The Maya Pill.*

TOMAŽ ŠALAMUN, *Soy Realidad.*

LYDIE SALVAYRE, *The Company of Ghosts.*
The Lecture.
The Power of Flies.

LUIS RAFAEL SÁNCHEZ, *Macho Camacho's Beat.*

SEVERO SARDUY, *Cobra & Maitreya.*

NATHALIE SARRAUTE, *Do You Hear Them?*
Martereau.
The Planetarium.

STIG SÆTERBAKKEN, *Siamese.*
Self-Control.
Through the Night.

ARNO SCHMIDT, *Collected Novellas.*
Collected Stories.
Nobodaddy's Children.
Two Novels.

ASAF SCHURR, *Motti.*

GAIL SCOTT, *My Paris.*

DAMION SEARLS, *What We Were Doing and Where We Were Going.*

JUNE AKERS SEESE,
Is This What Other Women Feel Too?

BERNARD SHARE, *Inish.*
Transit.

VIKTOR SHKLOVSKY, *Bowstring.*
Literature and Cinematography.
Theory of Prose.
Third Factory.
Zoo, or Letters Not about Love.

PIERRE SINIAC, *The Collaborators.*

KJERSTI A. SKOMSVOLD,
The Faster I Walk, the Smaller I Am.

JOSEF ŠKVORECKÝ, *The Engineer of Human Souls.*

GILBERT SORRENTINO, *Aberration of Starlight.*
Blue Pastoral.
Crystal Vision.

Imaginative Qualities of Actual Things.
Mulligan Stew. Red the Fiend.
Steelwork.
Under the Shadow.

MARKO SOSIČ, *Ballerina, Ballerina.*

ANDRZEJ STASIUK, *Dukla.*
Fado.

GERTRUDE STEIN, *The Making of Americans.*
A Novel of Thank You.

LARS SVENDSEN, *A Philosophy of Evil.*

PIOTR SZEWC, *Annihilation.*

GONÇALO M. TAVARES, *A Man: Klaus Klump.*
Jerusalem.
Learning to Pray in the Age of Technique.

LUCIAN DAN TEODOROVICI,
Our Circus Presents...

NIKANOR TERATOLOGEN, *Assisted Living.*

STEFAN THEMERSON, *Hobson's Island.*
The Mystery of the Sardine.
Tom Harris.

TAEKO TOMIOKA, *Building Waves.*

JOHN TOOMEY, *Sleepwalker.*

DUMITRU TSEPENEAG, *Hotel Europa.*
The Necessary Marriage.
Pigeon Post.
Vain Art of the Fugue.

ESTHER TUSQUETS, *Stranded.*

DUBRAVKA UGRESIC, *Lend Me Your Character.*
Thank You for Not Reading.

TOR ULVEN, *Replacement.*

MATI UNT, *Brecht at Night.*
Diary of a Blood Donor.
Things in the Night.

ÁLVARO URIBE & OLIVIA SEARS, EDS.,
Best of Contemporary Mexican Fiction.

ELOY URROZ, *Friction.*
The Obstacles.

LUISA VALENZUELA, *Dark Desires and the Others.*
He Who Searches.

PAUL VERHAEGHEN, *Omega Minor.*

BORIS VIAN, *Heartsnatcher.*

LLORENÇ VILLALONGA, *The Dolls' Room.*

TOOMAS VINT, *An Unending Landscape.*

ORNELA VORPSI, *The Country Where No One Ever Dies.*

AUSTRYN WAINHOUSE, *Hedyphagetica.*

CURTIS WHITE, *America's Magic Mountain.*
The Idea of Home.
Memories of My Father Watching TV.
Requiem.

DIANE WILLIAMS,
Excitability: Selected Stories.
Romancer Erector.

DOUGLAS WOOLF, *Wall to Wall.*
Ya! & John-Juan.

JAY WRIGHT, *Polynomials and Pollen.*
The Presentable Art of Reading Absence.

PHILIP WYLIE, *Generation of Vipers.*

MARGUERITE YOUNG, *Angel in the Forest.*
Miss MacIntosh, My Darling.

REYOUNG, *Unbabbling.*

VLADO ŽABOT, *The Succubus.*

ZORAN ŽIVKOVIĆ , *Hidden Camera.*

LOUIS ZUKOFSKY, *Collected Fiction.*

VITOMIL ZUPAN, *Minuet for Guitar.*

SCOTT ZWIREN, *God Head.*

AND MORE . . .